"Maybe we should set a few other ground rules if we're to be friends," Amy said.

David grinned at her. "Ones we can keep like the first rule or ones we can't?"

"No more kisses. I mean it," she sputtered. "It's just chemistry. Hormones. Pheromones."

"All of the above. But how does that stop me from wanting to haul you into my arms right now?"

"If we're able to ignore it, the temptation will eventually fade."

That raised his eyebrows. "If you believe that, I don't know how you ever got to be a psychologist."

"I can do anything I make up my mind to do," Amy said coolly.

She'd just laid down a challenge. David smiled. He hadn't felt like taking up any challenges for over a year, but he sure as hell meant to run with this one.

Dear Reader,

April may bring showers, but it also brings in a fabulous new batch of books from Silhouette Special Edition! This month treat yourself to the beginning of a brand-new exciting royal continuity, CROWN AND GLORY. We get the regal ball rolling with Laurie Paige's delightful tale *The Princess Is Pregnant!* This romance is fair to bursting with passion and other temptations.

I'm pleased to offer *The Groom's Stand-In* by Gina Wilkins— a fascinating story that is sure to keep readers on the edge of their seats…and warm their hearts in the process. Peggy Webb is no stranger herself to heartwarming romance with the next installment of her miniseries THE WESTMORELAND DIARIES. In *Force of Nature,* a beautiful photojournalist encounters a primitive man in the wilderness and must find a way to tame his oh-so-wild heart.

In *The Man in Charge*, Judith Lyons gives us a tender reunion romance where an endangered chancellor's daughter finds herself being guarded by the man she's never been able to forget—a rugged mercenary who's about to learn he's the father of their child! And in Wendy Warren's new sensation *Dakota Bride,* readers will relish the theme of learning to love again, as a young widow dreams of love and marriage with a handsome stranger. In addition, you'll find an intriguing case of mistaken identity in Jane Toombs's *Trouble in Tourmaline*, where a world-weary lawyer takes a breather from his fast-paced life and finds his sights brightened by a lovely psychologist, who takes him for a gardener. You won't want to put this story down!

So kick back and enjoy the fantasy of falling in love, and be sure to return next month for another winning selection of emotionally satisfying and uplifting stories of love, life and family!

Best,

Karen Taylor Richman
Senior Editor

Please address questions and book requests to:
Silhouette Reader Service
U.S.: 3010 Walden Ave., P.O. Box 1325, Buffalo, NY 14269
Canadian: P.O. Box 609, Fort Erie, Ont. L2A 5X3

Trouble in Tourmaline

JANE TOOMBS

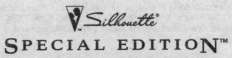

SPECIAL EDITION™

Published by Silhouette Books

America's Publisher of Contemporary Romance

To:
My son-in-law Steve, the lawyer
My grand-nephew Dale, the psychologist
My friend Denny, the psychiatrist
My five-year-old violinist granddaughter, Kate

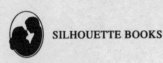

SILHOUETTE BOOKS

ISBN 0-373-24464-9

TROUBLE IN TOURMALINE

Copyright © 2002 by Jane Toombs

Visit Silhouette at www.eHarlequin.com

Printed in U.S.A.

Books by Jane Toombs

Silhouette Special Edition

Nobody's Baby #1081
Baby of Mine #1182
Accidental Parents #1247
Designated Daddy #1271
Wild Mustang #1326
Her Mysterious Houseguest #1391
The Missing Heir #1432
Trouble in Tourmaline #1464

Silhouette Shadows

Return to Bloodstone House #5
Dark Enchantment #12
What Waits Below #16
The Volan Curse #35
The Woman in White #50
The Abandoned Bride #56

Previously published under the pseudonym Diana Stuart

Silhouette Special Edition

Out of a Dream #353
The Moon Pool #671

Silhouette Desire

Prime Specimen #172
Leader of the Pack #238
The Shadow Between #257

JANE TOOMBS

lives most of the year on the shore of Lake Superior in Michigan's Upper Peninsula along with a man from her past and their crazy calico cat, Kinko. In the winter, though, they all defect to Florida for three months. In addition to writing, Jane enjoys knitting and gardening.

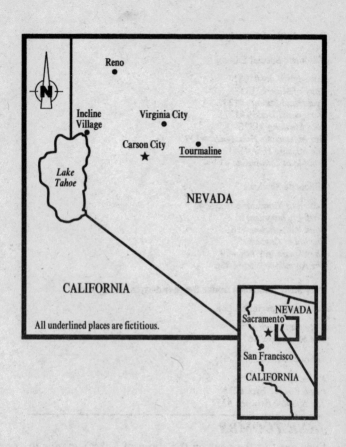

Reno

Incline
Village

Virginia City

Carson City
Tourmaline

Lake
Tahoe

NEVADA

CALIFORNIA

All underlined places are fictitious.

NEVADA
Sacramento

San Francisco

CALIFORNIA

Chapter One

David Severin parked the Tourmaline Nursery truck he'd borrowed in front of his aunt Gert's old Victorian home/office and began unloading lilac and forsythia shrubs. Late May being warm in the high desert of northern Nevada, he shed his T-shirt, wishing he'd put on shorts rather than jeans. He knew very well his psychiatrist aunt's insistence that he do a complete revamp of her landscaping was no more than a psychological ploy to get him out sweating in the fresh air, but what the hell, at least she wasn't trying to psychoanalyze him. Actually, he was enjoying the work as much as he'd enjoyed anything in the past year, so maybe she knew what she was doing.

Yesterday he'd dug up an old hedge and hauled the scraggly looking shrubs away. Now he needed to dump some topsoil in the deep trench he'd had to dig and then put in these new ones. After he finished with the topsoil, David noticed a fine layer of dirt clinging to his sweaty torso, so he strode over to the hose and sprayed himself clean. He was shutting the water off when a woman's voice said, "Excuse me."

Turning, he saw a stunning blonde in a pale blue suit that skimmed all the right places. She gazed at him with eyes as green as the forsythia leaves, asking, "Is this Dr. Severin's office?"

Realizing belatedly he'd been staring at her like a thirsty man at a cool drink, he gathered his wits. He figured she might be what Gert called a detail person from a drug company, wanting his aunt to try some new antidepressant, or she could be a patient. Either way, she was out of luck.

He spoke brusquely to cover his momentary lapse. "The doctor isn't in town, won't be back for two days."

"Oh." He could hear the disappointment in her voice.

Maybe she *was* a patient, in which case he ought to try to help her. Reluctantly—he was definitely not ready to get even minimally involved with a woman right now—he muttered, "Is there anything I can do?"

Her gaze drifted over him and she hesitated for a long moment. "Is there a good place in town to get a sandwich and a cold drink?"

From out of town, then. Gert had quite a few patients who were. He hadn't heard a car drive up earlier, so he glanced around, noticing a blue SUV parked so closely behind the nursery truck that he wasn't sure they weren't touching.

"The best place is hard to find," he said more gruffly than he intended, still wondering whether she had, in fact, hit the back of his truck.

"I can follow directions." Her tart tone amused him, snapping her back into focus.

"This is a well hidden hole-in-the-wall. Easier to walk there from here than drive."

"I'm capable of walking." This time her words held a definite edge, which, for some reason, made him ignore his uneasiness at being attracted to her.

"Easier to show you than tell you," he said.

Amy Simon eyed the dark-haired man uncertainly as he grabbed a T-shirt from the porch railing and yanked it over his head. In the back of her mind she thought it was a shame to cover that muscular torso glistening with droplets of water. Definitely a hunk. No wonder she'd been momentarily attracted—any woman would have been—until his brusque manner turned her off. Now he was practically ordering her to go with him to wherever the hole-in-the-wall was, something she didn't care for, either. It reminded her unpleasantly of the psychologist who'd been monitoring her in L.A. Her grandmother would have called Dr. Smits a little tin god on wheels. Smits was a good part of the reason she'd opted to answer Dr. Severin's ad for a psychologist.

But this guy wasn't Smits, and she *was* hungry and thirsty. A walk would do her good after the drive over here from her brother's horse ranch in Carson Valley, where she'd spent the night. "Thank you," she said finally. Hoping to pry a name out of him, she added, "I'm Amy, by the way."

"David," he told her, and started down the sidewalk, away from where her car was parked.

She followed, hurrying to keep up with him. David? She'd have thought a yard maintenance worker would go by something more macho, like Dave. Immediately she made a face. Shame on her, that was stereotyping, something she'd thought all those psych courses had taught her not to do.

He strode along without talking. Strong silent type? More than likely he had nothing intelligent to say. Oops, more typecasting. Why did she keep downgrading the guy? Could it be because she didn't want to acknowledge that he turned her on? But that would make her a snob, wouldn't it? Deciding conversation would dispel such disturbing thoughts, Amy cleared her throat and asked, "Did you grow up in Tourmaline?"

"No."

"Nevada?"

"No."

Tamping down exasperation, she persisted. "Where, then?"

"New Mexico."

End of conversation, as far as he was concerned, apparently. She lost count of the corners they'd turned when he finally stopped, turned and looked at her. His eyes, she noted, were as dark a blue as she'd ever seen. They revealed nothing.

"Why?" he asked.

She blinked, finally understanding he must mean

why did she want to know where he grew up. "I was just making small talk," she muttered.

"This is it." He gestured toward a green door. The sign over it read Tiny Tim's. Opening the door, he waved her in ahead of him.

Four minuscule tables were crowded into the small space inside. When they were seated at number two, the only empty one, David said, "Your turn."

To do what? Order? Talk? She shrugged.

"What state?" he asked.

Oh, where had she grown up. "Michigan," she told him.

"Not a real good way to start a conversation," he said.

"Whatcha having?" a gruff voice asked.

Turning her head, she saw a bald man's head framed in an open hatch on the side wall.

"Got a special, Tim?" David asked.

"Egg salad with alfalfa sprouts, mustard and pickle on rye."

David glanced at her and she nodded. It sounded sort of weird, but so was the day, so far. "Root beer's good, they make it locally," he added.

Not what she'd usually order, but she decided to go with the flow. "Okay."

Tim's head disappeared from view.

"So what is your idea of a good conversation starter?" she asked David, trying to ignore how really small their table was. It was impossible to move without her feet or legs brushing against his, each touch heightening her awareness of the sizzle arcing between them.

David looked across the table into her green eyes. Murdock, the senior partner of the law firm he used to be with, had green eyes. Murdock's were a murky color, though, like his manipulations had turned out to be. Amy's eyes were clear and filled with light, enhancing her heart-shaped face. No doubt about it, she was the prettiest woman he'd seen in a long time, with a lower lip that begged for... He forced his gaze away, telling himself he wasn't going down that road. Even if the air between them was all but crackling with electricity.

What had she asked him? Before he could bring it to mind, she spoke. "I've never been in favor of starting out by asking what someone does for a living. The emphasis then tends to be on what you do rather than what you're like."

"Fine with me. So what do you think I'm like?"

"You're supposed to tell me."

He shook his head.

"Table two, yours is ready," Tim said from the open hatch.

David rose, retrieved the tray from the shelf below the hatch, brought it back to the table and served them both, then slid the tray back onto the counter.

He took a bite of his sandwich, chewed and swallowed, washing it down with a slug of root beer. "I always figured people show enough of what they're like, so you get clues," he said. "Take you—I already know you don't live in Tourmaline and that you're an honest Midwesterner."

Amy's laugh was unexpectedly deep, charming

him against his will. "Where'd you get the idea Midwesterners were more honest than anyone else?"

"From TV, where else?"

She rolled her eyes. "All right, then, from clues I know you're either a landscaper or that you work for one. But I certainly have no notion of whether New Mexicans are more or less honest that Midwesterners."

With Murdock in mind, his "Definitely less" came out tinged with bitterness, which vanished when the rest of what she'd said filtered in. This woman thought he was Gert's yardman? He half smiled. Wasn't she right in a sense? He hadn't done any kind of work in more than a year other than mowing his aunt's lawn and keeping the shrubs trimmed and the weeds under control. Why not play the part? Besides, he could use a little fun in his life.

Without saying one way or the other whether Amy was right or wrong, David finished his sandwich and drink. Since she was through eating at about the same time, he gathered she really had been hungry.

"You know, that weird sandwich wasn't bad," she told him. "And I haven't had root beer in years. Thanks for letting me know about this place." She reached into her purse and removed a wallet.

David quelled his impulse to offer to pay for hers as well as his, deciding that Aunt Gert's yardman wouldn't. Dutch it'd be. He thought of Cal, the worker who'd helped him load the shrubs at the nursery. Though he didn't own a baseball cap, he could adopt Cal's swagger and mannerisms.

"Rather have a beer," he told Amy, getting out his own wallet, "but Tim doesn't sell the stuff."

"Oh. Um, so do you have a dog?" she asked, another lame attempt at small talk with the handyman.

Actually he'd just acquired a cat, a stray that had meowed so persistently at his apartment door one night a week ago that he'd let the animal in. When Gert saw her she told him the cat was pregnant. Soon he'd have kittens. A case of no good deed going unpunished.

Cats and kittens didn't suit the role he'd decided to play, so, remembering something Cal had said, David decided to use it. "Had two dogs," he told her. "Rottweilers. Some rotten dipstick stole 'em right out of my pickup."

"What a shame."

"Yeah, you'd think they'd've put up a fight. Who ever heard of wimpy rottweilers? Just as well they're gone."

He could tell by her quickly masked expression that he was rapidly turning her off. Which was what he wanted, wasn't it?

The bill taken care of, they left the café and walked back toward Aunt Gert's.

"You said Dr. Severin won't be home for two days?" Amy asked.

"That's what she told me."

"I suppose I should have called ahead."

He stated the obvious, which she ought to know if she was a patient. "The doc works by the appointment system."

"Well, yes, but I was hoping…" She let the words trail off.

Maybe she was a new patient and had hoped Gert could work her in. What could Amy's problem be? She didn't seem depressed, and he ought to know depression when he saw it—he was an expert.

"I guess I'll just stay over," she said. "Is there a quiet place in town?"

An arousing mental picture of Amy naked in his bed tonight flashed into his head, but he resisted the temptation to tell her his apartment was about as quiet as it got. To banish the vision, he said tersely, "The local hotel's not bad."

"What's 'not bad' mean?"

She never let anything alone, did she? "It's old but clean. Serves a decent meal, and it's quiet."

"Where is it?"

"I'll show you."

She stopped and looked up at him. "Maybe you could just tell me."

Obviously he'd overdone the Cal routine. Now he was stuck with it. Deliberately ignoring her words, he said, "The hotel is up this way," then took her elbow to turn her to the left, which was a mistake. He hadn't actually touched her before, and, if he'd sensed the electricity between them in the café, he damn well felt it now.

For a moment neither of them moved, then she jerked free, frowning at him.

He gave her a one-sided smile. "Coming?"

He thought she might not, but then she fell into

step beside him. "Shouldn't you get back to your job?"

"Hey, it's my lunch break."

The Cottonwood Hotel was in the next block and nothing more was said until they reached the front entrance. She stopped and peered inside. "It's got slot machines," she said accusingly. "That's not quiet."

"Most commercial places in Nevada have slots. Take another look. You see anyone playing those machines?"

"Not at the moment."

"No smoking."

"What's that supposed to mean?"

"Gamblers are mostly smokers. Old Hathaway, who owns the place, won't let anyone smoke inside his hotel. The hard-case gamblers go where they can."

Amy raised her eyebrows, hesitated, then said, "I suppose I can give it a try. Goodbye and thanks." Without giving him a chance to respond, she pushed open the door to the lobby and slipped through it into the hotel.

That was that, David told himself as he sauntered back toward Aunt Gert's. A brief encounter and a goodbye. The end. Well, it was fun while it lasted.

Before he'd gotten half a block away, he saw Hal Hathaway coming toward him. "Just sent you a customer," he told Hal.

Hal stopped beside him. "I certainly can use all you send me. I hope this one is pretty."

David nodded. No argument there.

"Is your aunt back yet?" Hal asked.

"Not until the day after tomorrow."

"The reason is, I've been wanting to ask her if she wants that vacant lot on the street directly in back of you. I've decided to sell and she gets first refusal."

"I don't know. You'll have to ask her."

Hal went on to list all the reasons why Gert should buy the lot, then remembered something in the hotel basement he wanted to show David.

When David finally was able to get away, he shook his head. He liked the old man, but he was sure long-winded. By the time he got back to his aunt's, the blue SUV in back of the nursery truck was gone. The time he'd spent with Hal had given Amy long enough to walk to Gert's and drive the SUV back to the hotel parking lot. He'd missed a last goodbye.

Or would it have been one? If Amy was a patient of Gert's he might run into her sometime. Best to stay away from his aunt's patients, though. He didn't need anyone else's problems while he was still struggling with his own.

He'd have to consider the fact he usually ate breakfast at the Cottonwood. Giving it a miss for the next two mornings would be a good idea. When he went to bed that night, he kept the thought in mind and wound up dreaming he was in a Manhattan theater watching a follies-type stage show, especially the chorus girl on the left end of the row. He was seated close to her, so close he could see her eyes were green, though her eyes weren't what he was paying the most attention to....

While shaving early the next morning, he told himself he damn well wasn't going to change his routine on the off chance he might run into Amy. She'd probably sleep late and no place in town served a better breakfast.

Amy woke at her usual hour and groaned. Here she was more or less on vacation for today and could have slept in. As always, once awake, hunger stalked her. She could never understand those who made do with just orange juice or coffee for breakfast, she needed a meal. David had been right when he said the hotel served decent food—dinner had been delicious. She looked forward to breakfast.

David. Why was he still on her mind? At least she hadn't dreamed about him. Not that she could recall, anyway. Being a psychologist, she did try to track her dreams, but, oddly enough, couldn't remember any this morning. Perhaps she'd suppressed them and she actually *had* dreamed of David. There's an unsettling thought.

Actually she probably would see him again, however briefly, because the yard work Dr. Severin was having done had looked quite extensive, but it'd be no more than a "Hi" sort of encounter. The last thing she needed at the moment was a man in her life. Never mind what Dr. Smits had told her about her denial state where men were concerned. He was another example of a controlling man himself. Sometimes she wondered how his wife could stand him.

On the off chance that Dr. Severin might come home earlier than expected, Amy put on a dark green skirt with a lighter green shirt, ran a brush through her short curly hair and left her room.

As she entered the dining room, she noticed the waitress seating a man—David. Annoyed because her heart gave a lurch, she wished she could walk past him without a word, but that would be confirming Smits' diagnosis of denial. Okay, she'd acknowledge David's presence by a courteous hello. Why was she making such a big deal of it, anyway?

The waitress came to seat her and Amy was almost at his table when he saw her. He stood up, unsmiling, and gestured toward an empty chair.

"I guess you're with David," the waitress said, plopping the menu she held onto his table. "I'm Vera and I'll be right back."

Telling herself it'd be awkward to back out, Amy let David seat her.

"You didn't tell me you ate breakfast here," she said.

"I expected you to sleep late," he told her.

"Why?"

He shrugged.

"Do I impress you as someone who doesn't work for a living?" she asked.

He shrugged again.

Realizing she sounded defensive, which would never do, Amy took a deep breath and decided to start over. "Good morning, David."

His lips curved slightly, not quite a smile. "'Morning, Amy."

"I see the sun is out."

"Usually is in May hereabouts."

"You don't make small talk easy."

"I don't?" His gaze met hers.

The deep blue of his eyes fascinated her. What color were they? Darker than cobalt or azure, but lighter than navy. They dominated his face, making it difficult for her to look away. When she forced herself to, she found herself examining the curve of his upper lip. He had a rather full mouth, as she did. She found his attractive. What would it be like to feel those lips touching hers?

Wrong place to go. "Once I wake up I'm hungry," she blurted, throwing the words at him as a barrier.

"Likewise, I'm sure. Coffee, then food, fast. You?" When she nodded, he lifted the coffee server and poured some into her cup.

"Thanks." She took a swallow. As she remembered from last night, it was excellent.

"Black's the only way to drink it." He actually sounded approving.

To discourage any more approval, remembering his comment about beer the day before, she said, "I don't like beer in any way, shape or form."

He raised an eyebrow. "What's beer got to do with coffee?"

"Nothing much, you ask me," Vera, the waitress, told him, having arrived unobserved. "You guys ready to order?"

When she'd taken their order and left, David said, "Vera said it all. Beer and coffee, apples and oranges."

He really did have a habit of picking every comment apart, didn't he? Two could play that game. "So you decided you weren't likely to run into me at breakfast since I was obviously a late sleeper."

"Can't be right all the time. Figured you didn't have anything to get up for this morning. Didn't tie in hunger."

Something flashed into his eyes as he said the last word, but it was gone before she could be sure what she'd seen. A different kind of hunger? Damn chemistry, anyway—she could feel the tension between them like a palpable chain. He certainly gave off irresistible pheromones. Or was it only females who did that? Looking at him across the table seemed to be turning her brain to mush.

David tried to focus on his coffee, but he couldn't keep his gaze away from her. Today she wore a skirt and a polo shirt, green like those deep-sea eyes of hers. A bad mistake to come here for breakfast. He should have stayed away. Far away.

No woman had tempted him for more than a second or two since his divorce, but he couldn't make himself ignore Amy. While any man would give her a second look, this was more than reacting to a pretty face atop a well-built body. He seemed to be drawn to her in a way that scared the hell out of him.

Vera's arrival with their food was a welcome break. He wondered if it was for Amy, too, since she concentrated on her food and didn't talk. If she didn't want to sit with him, why hadn't she declined his offer to share a table? For that matter, why had he made it? Courtesy? He knew better.

Yeah, Severin, and you know better than to get into a tangle you'll regret.

He tried to come up with something Cal might say, something that might turn her completely off him, and found all he could think of was that Cal was actually an all-right guy. What he'd been doing was parodying Cal's speech patterns and making a mockery of the guy's lifestyle. He scowled.

"Is something wrong with your food?" Amy asked.

He glanced up at her. "Why?"

"You've been glaring down at your plate forever."

"The food's fine."

"Oh, then it must be the company you're annoyed with."

"I asked for the company, didn't I?"

She raised her eyebrows. "That doesn't mean you can't have regrets."

"If I'm annoyed at anyone, it's myself." He picked up his cup, downed the last drop of coffee and reached for the carafe. "Care for a refill?"

"Just warm it, thanks." She waited until he poured more coffee into her cup, then said, "Anger's destructive."

"So I've been told." By his aunt, more than once in the past year. He poured himself another cupful and took a swallow. Been told that and other cautions he hadn't wanted to hear. *Ethically,* Gert wasn't allowed to psychoanalyze him because he was a relative. Which didn't prevent her from dropping loaded hints. Or making a yardman out of him, like Amy believed he was. The last thought made him smile.

"That's better," she said.

"You catch more flies with honey than vinegar, too," he deadpanned.

"Always supposing you're looking to catch flies." Her words challenged him.

"I'm not looking to catch anything." He spoke flatly, his gaze crossing hers.

He watched her face turn expressionless, but her tone was light when she said, "And here I felt sure you were a fisherman."

"Every yardman doesn't fish."

He could see he'd managed to offend her. "I was not trying to categorize you," she snapped.

He glanced at the egg congealing on his plate and knew he couldn't finish his breakfast. Just as well, because this seemed a good time to split. He flipped a couple of bucks on the table for a tip, rose, nodded to her and walked to the cashier to pay his bill. Not hers, though it might annoy her more if he did. But he figured he'd done enough damage. He was safe. Amy wasn't likely to give him the time of day again, even if she became a regular patient of his aunt's. Just the way he wanted it.

Then why didn't he feel relieved?

Amy watched David leave the hotel, then pushed her plate to one side, her appetite gone. What a boor. Though she hadn't wanted to explore what might have been between them any more than he did, he didn't need to be so abrupt. With time maybe they could have managed to become friends.

Friends? Ha. Who was she trying to snow? Hadn't she learned not to fool herself? If anything had ever been going to happen between her and David, it wouldn't be friendship. She'd never gone in for brief, hot affairs—like any relationship with him would have been—so it was just as well their acquaintance had ended on a sour note.

She should be glad. She was glad. With luck he'd finish the yard work at Dr. Severin's quickly and then be out of her life completely. He was as forgettable as any other man.

And if he knew what was good for him, he'd better keep out of her dreams, too.

Chapter Two

Cal was unloading a new batch of greenery from the nursery truck when David reached Aunt Gert's.

"Wanted to be sure you got the rest of the stuff you need early," Cal said.

"Thanks." David pitched in to help, thinking again of how he'd used Cal. What he'd done wouldn't harm Cal in any way, but he was unpleasantly reminded of how Murdock had patronized him last year. In no way, shape or form did he want to be like that bastard.

"The boss says you ever want a job, just ask," Cal told him when they finished. "He drove by yesterday while you was putting in them shrubs. Said you're a damn good worker."

"Tell him I appreciate the compliment." Which was the truth. Not that he intended to do landscaping for a living.

David watched Cal pull away in the truck. In a way, he envied the man. Cal liked his job and seemed to be satisfied with his life, which was a hell of a lot more than could be said about David Severin. He lived comfortably enough, having been lucky enough to put the money his grandfather had left him in investments that proved both sound and profitable. Still, he was getting restless doing nothing. Aunt Gert had urged him to take both the Nevada bar exams, which he'd passed, but he had no heart for law after what had happened in New Mexico. The truth was, he didn't know what he wanted to do with the rest of his life.

A few plantings later, his gloomy mood began to lift. Gert was right about hard work in the open air easing depression. He peeled off his T-shirt, hung it on the porch railing and picked up a spirea bush. He'd just finished digging the hole for it when he saw Gert's car pulling into the drive. She waved at him on her way back to the garage. He dropped the bush into the hole, quickly covered the roots and set aside the spade.

As he walked toward the garage, the overhead door went down and Gert emerged from the side door, carrying a small overnight case.

"You're home early," he told her. "Let me take that inside for you."

She handed him the case. "A delegation from the Walker Valley reservation called on Grandfather, wanting advice. What they really wanted, I soon saw, was for him to go back there with them, so I gracefully bowed out."

David knew she meant her friend, a Paiute medicine man who insisted everyone call him Grandfather.

She stopped in the utility room and told him to leave the case by the washer. "He'd had one of his dreams, by the way," she said. "Something about two red-tailed hawks. You were one of them, apparently."

Since Grandfather's dreams often had some bearing on reality, David waited for her to go on. Instead, she switched subjects. "Now I'm going to take a shower, change and come sit on the front porch and watch you work."

"The hawks?"

"I'm still thinking about that dream. When I have it figured out I'll let you know." She left him in the utility room.

David retraced his steps out the back door and around to the front again. He picked up the spade and set to work once more. He'd gotten more than half the plantings in when his aunt appeared on the porch with a pitcher of limeade and two glasses.

"Join me?" she invited.

After using the hose to wash some of the dirt off his bare skin, he donned his T-shirt and took a chair beside his aunt, who was sitting on the glider, moving gently back and forth. He reached for the drink she'd poured for him and swallowed half the contents of the tall glass.

"This is hand-squeezed limeade," his aunt said. "You're supposed to sip and savor the result of my efforts."

"Too thirsty." The words reminded him of his first

sight of Amy. "By the way, someone came by yesterday to see you—I think she might have been a new patient. I told her you'd be back tomorrow."

"All my regulars knew I was out of town," Gert said.

David leaned back in the chair, stretching out his legs. Felt good to take a break. Like yesterday when he'd had lunch with Amy at Tiny Tim's. He closed his eyes and there she was in her blue suit, the way he'd seen her that day...

"Penny for your thoughts," Gert said. "They must be pleasant, since you're smiling."

Without opening his eyes he told a half-truth. "Just relaxed."

Still thinking about yesterday, he was falling into a half doze when Gert exclaimed, "Why, look who's here. You've come early."

David's eyes popped open and for a moment he thought he was having a vision straight out of his daydream. Amy was climbing the front steps to the porch. He stumbled to his feet, unable to believe his eyes.

"I know I wasn't supposed to be here until tomorrow, Dr. Severin," Amy said. "I'm sorry if I've inconvenienced you." She didn't look at him.

"Not a bit. I'm just glad I came home a day early," Gert said. "Amy, this is my nephew, David Severin. David, Amy Simon, whom I told you would be coming to work with me."

It all came back to him then. Dr. Simon, Gert had said, was finishing up her probationary year toward getting her license, in which she had to be under the supervision of a licensed psychologist or a board-certified psychiatrist. He'd remembered Dr. Simon was female, but he'd forgotten her first name. He'd assumed she'd be older. And definitely not a sexy blonde.

"Hello, Mr. Severin," Amy said, those green eyes of hers as cold as the limeade he'd downed.

He swallowed and inclined his head. "Dr. Simon."

"Heavens, such formality," his aunt said, giving him an odd look. "I'm Gert, she's Amy and you're David."

"Yes," he muttered, "she's Amy, all right."

"And you're David." Amy's voice was as frosty as her eyes.

Gert rose from the glider to look at one, then the other of them. "Such antipathy can only mean, I do believe, that you've met before. This does explain at least part of Grandfather's dream about the male hawk and the female hawk."

Recovering somewhat from the shock of discovering David was Dr. Severin's nephew, Amy was confused anew by his aunt's words. Gert had to be in her seventies and she had a grandfather? Good grief, how old would he be?

"I'm forgetting my manners," Gert said to her. "As I mentioned when we had that brief meeting in Reno last month, you'll stay with me until you find a place to live. Do come in and I'll show you to your room."

"Well, um, I'm at the Cottonwood Hotel at the moment." The last place Amy wanted to stay was anywhere David might be living.

Apparently sensing this, Gert said, "David has his own apartment to the west of town so you don't need to worry about putting him out. It'll be handier for you here than at the hotel until you find a place of your own."

Which was true. Especially if David planned to eat breakfast at the Cottonwood every morning. "It's very kind of you, Dr.—"

"Didn't I just say the name is Gert?"

Amy managed a smile, beginning to feel she was going to get along with her new employer. "Thanks, Gert."

"This yardman better get back to work," David said.

Amy slanted him a dirty look. Sure, rub it in, she thought, when you deliberately let me believe that's what you were. She wondered why he didn't explain himself right away.

"Amy may need some help transferring her things from the hotel," Gert reminded David.

"No!" Amy cried. "That is, I mean I wouldn't dream of bothering him when I'm perfectly capable of doing it on my own."

Gert's dark gaze assessed her. "I see I'm odd woman out at this rather peculiar interchange. Since I'm related to one of you and have invited the other to be my new associate, don't you think I deserve an explanation?"

After a long moment of silence, David said, "She's the one I thought might be a new patient of yours."

Gert turned from him to Amy. "Apparently you didn't tell him your name?"

"She said it was Amy," David admitted. "I'd forgotten Dr. Simon's first name, so I didn't make the connection."

"He told me he was David," Amy confessed. "Since I had no other identification to go by, I'm afraid I thought he was your yardman."

Gert's chuckle turned into whoops of laughter.

Amy looked at David, who shrugged, but she thought she detected a quiver of a beginning smile. Maybe it *was* funny. Maybe she'd think so next year. Or the year after. She didn't at the moment. He'd led her on, she was sure, once she'd mentioned she thought he worked for a landscaper. Come to think of it, hadn't it been just after that he'd mentioned the wimpy rottweilers and wanting a beer?

So annoyed she couldn't hold her tongue, she scowled at him and muttered, "I'll bet you never did own a dog, let alone two."

Raising her eyebrows, Gert said, "He does have a cat—and maybe even kittens by now."

To Amy's surprise, David grinned at her. "No dogs, and I admit I'm not really into beer, either. Truce. After all, you didn't let on who you were, either."

Now he was trying to charm her. She wasn't going to fall for that, but, because she was to be his aunt's associate, Amy squashed down her irritation. She didn't have to like him, but, since he was Gert's nephew, she should try to be courteous. "You have a cat?" she asked.

"You could say she picked me."

"Kittens are imminent," Gert added. "Now that

we have the fuss momentarily settled, do come inside, Amy.''

After the two of them went into the house, David walked down the porch steps and picked up the shovel. Amy's SUV was parked in front of his pickup at curbside and he could see what the truck had hid yesterday. A California license. Maybe that would have given him a clue to her identity. And maybe not. Even though he knew he'd improved, he still wasn't focused as well as he used to be a year ago. Betrayal by two of the people he trusted most—his boss and his wife—had knocked him off-kilter.

As he was wrestling a large oleander into the ground, Amy came onto the porch and stood for a moment, her gaze on him. He was tempted to ask if she enjoyed watching the yardman, but decided she was peeved enough with him already. He was tamping the dirt down when she descended the steps. Would she walk past without acknowledging his existence?

''So you took a stray cat in,'' she said. ''A stray pregnant cat.''

He set the shovel aside. ''The cat kept pestering me.''

''Nevertheless, it helped me decide that we should start over with our formal introduction of today and put the past behind us.''

''You mean yesterday and this morning at breakfast?''

''That's the past, isn't it?''

Her snappishness amused him. Either she riled easily, or, as he suspected, he was the cause. "Become friends, you mean?"

She hesitated. "Well, I suppose you could put it like that."

Reminded of a court case in New Mexico, David chuckled.

"What's so funny?" she demanded.

He decided to tell her. "I once watched while a judge lectured two men in court about one assaulting the other with a paintbrush loaded with paint. Apparently one had been criticizing how the other was painting a fence. The painter took it for a while, but finally turned and swiped the paintbrush across the other man's face. The judge told them they were wasting the court's time and ordered them to shake hands and be friends again." He paused.

"So they did?"

"You don't argue with a judge's decision. 'Me, I do that, Your Honor,' the painter said, 'but I tell by the look in his eye, he no be friends with me.'"

A reluctant smile crept across Amy's face. "You caught me. I really didn't mean friends, but I'm willing to try." She stepped off the sidewalk over to where he stood, and offered her hand.

David clasped it in his, holding it while the potency of what had been between them from the beginning jolted through him. From the sudden widening of her eyes, he suspected she felt it, too. Back to square one.

As their hands parted, he said, "Friends," very much aware that friendship wasn't all he wanted from Amy.

Amy got into her SUV and drove toward the hotel,

wondering just what she'd promised to David with that handshake. Actually they'd held hands, rather than shaken them, and when they finally let go, she hadn't wanted to. What was it about the man that drew her? Sure, he was a hunk, but she'd met hunks before without her hormones acting up.

She remembered what her brother, Russ, had told her about his first meeting with Mari, now his wife. "She was sitting on a corral fence. She took off her hat and I saw this glorious hair and knew right then I was a goner. Especially since I'd already noticed her cute butt."

David *did* have a cute butt. The thought made her laugh. She was overreacting to a purely chemical attraction, something she'd certainly get over. Especially since she intended to be too busy to spend much time with her new "friend."

At the hotel, the lobby was empty. Mr. Hathaway, a short, stout man with white hair, was at the desk. "Checking out, are you?" he asked. "I hope you were happy here."

"You have a nice quiet place," she told him. "And delicious food."

He beamed at her. "I do try to satisfy folks. I hope you'll dine with us again. I say that because I understand you had breakfast with David Severin, so I expect you may be around for a while. I heard Dr. Gert was taking on a female associate, and I figure you might be her."

Tourmaline was a small town, Amy reminded herself. Word got around small towns with the speed of light. "Yes, you're right."

"David's a nice young man. Too bad about that trouble he had in New Mexico. Can't believe any of it was his fault. His wife must have, though, because she divorced him."

A divorce? Amy was torn between not wanting to listen to gossip and finding out as much as she could about David. Her better nature lost. "A shame," she said. She had no clue what the trouble Mr. Hathaway was talking about might be, but she knew pumps needed priming.

"He wasn't disbarred, you know, so others in New Mexico must have felt he wasn't guilty."

David was a lawyer? All the more reason to stay clear of him. Since she hadn't any idea what had happened, she said nothing, merely nodded at Mr. Hathaway, hoping he'd tell her more.

"Women are like that," he said. "Desert a man just when he most needs support." She must have frowned, because he added quickly, "Don't mean you, of course. Or Dr. Gert, come to think of it. I amend my statement to say *some* women are like that, my ex-wife included."

She waited, but apparently his gaffe had rattled him into giving no more information about David's past. "It's been nice talking to you," she told him.

He winked at her. "Always have time for a pretty girl."

As Amy drove toward Gert's, she mulled over what she'd heard about David. He'd obviously been practicing law in New Mexico and had gotten into some kind of legal trouble there. It hadn't been serious enough to get him disbarred, but had evidently caused his wife to divorce him. She knew she wouldn't be satisfied until she learned more, but who to ask? Certainly not his aunt. Or, heaven forbid, David.

Was he practicing law here? The massive landscaping overhaul he was doing single-handedly at Gert's seemed to argue against it. Still, he could've taken time off.

Gert had told her to pull her vehicle into the drive past the house and park it where an extra cement slab had been laid down. Amy was grateful she'd be able to use the back door, thus avoiding David offering to help her move her things in.

When Amy was through settling her belongings into her bedroom and had changed into jeans and a polo shirt, she went downstairs to the office where she knew Gert would be. As she walked into the waiting room, Gert was just putting the phone down. She gestured Amy to a seat.

"That was Hal Hathaway, thanking me for choosing a young, good-looking associate. He thinks the town has enough old fogies as it is."

"News travels fast in Tourmaline," Amy said.

"Hal makes sure of that. He's the town's prime gossip. I assume he got his chance to talk to you when you checked out of his hotel."

Amy nodded.

"I'm sure he told you some things about David. How much?"

"Well, that David was divorced and there'd been some kind of a problem in New Mexico."

"Over a year ago, yes. David was at a low point when he came here. I felt he needed some therapy, but being a relative, it wasn't ethical for me to treat him. I tried to get him to go to a psychiatrist in Reno, but he refused. I have little doubt that he would have refused therapy even from me, had I been able to offer it."

"I don't know him well," Amy said cautiously, "but he doesn't seem to be in a depression now."

"Hard work in the sun and fresh air has been good medicine."

"The landscaping," Amy murmured.

"Exactly."

"Mr. Hathaway mentioned David was a lawyer."

"Is. He passed both Nevada bar exams." Gert sighed. "I remember him telling me when he was ten that when he grew up he was going to be a lawyer and help people, just like I was a doctor and helped them. Law was his dream. But now—" She paused and shook her head. "He's disillusioned with the profession. Who knows if he'll ever go back."

"If he passed the exams...?"

"I think he took them just to shut me up."

"He's in denial." It wasn't a question, Amy was offering a diagnosis.

Gert shrugged. "I've told you this because I know you'll hear more gossip. I also realize that you and David got off on the wrong foot. He'll work things out eventually. Try not to be too hard on him."

"No, of course not." Even as Amy said the words, a plan was forming in her mind. Though she was Gert's associate, she wasn't related to David, so it wasn't exactly unethical for her to try to help him. Not that she'd be overt. With his negative attitude toward therapy, it'd never do to let him realize she was going to be attempting to steer him into overcoming his denial, so he could return to the profession he'd once loved.

She felt really noble for about ten seconds. Then it hit her. She, who had absolutely no use for the legal profession, was going to try to find a way to get this man to embrace law again? What a crock. On the other hand, she'd gone into psychology because she wanted to help people understand their problems and overcome them. David had a real problem. It shouldn't matter what it was, she was a psychologist and it was her duty to help him face up to his.

Should she discuss it with Gert? For a moment or two she wavered, then decided actually there was no need to, since she wasn't going to officially be David's therapist. Hers would be a covert operation. If it didn't work, no harm would come to him. There was a good chance she could pull it off, in which case he'd be better.

"Given time, I believe David and I can become friends," she said.

Gert smiled at her. "I hope so. Now I'll show you around a bit so you'll know where everything is when we start seeing patients tomorrow."

David, T-shirt slung on the porch rail again, inserted the last of today's shrubs into its hole, a hibiscus the nursery owner thought was hardy enough to survive a Nevada winter. Time would tell. He'd given it a southern exposure near the house so the plant would have a fighting chance.

"So are you through for the day?" Amy's voice came from behind, startling him.

He turned to look at her. "More or less."

"I've been thinking about our contract—you know, to try to be friends. It occurred to me if you don't know much about cats, I might be of some help when yours delivers her kittens. My mother always had cats, so I got to be an amateur expert in kittens at an early age."

Taken aback at her friendly offer, David hesitated, finally saying, "It's true I don't know much about cats."

"Most of them just go ahead and have their kittens, but some can be difficult about it. I could come over and meet her so she'll know me when the time comes."

Come to his apartment? He stared at her. What had brought on this sudden switch? She couldn't be coming on to him, so just what was she up to?

"Just to meet your cat, I mean." A tinge of coolness in her voice told him that Amy hadn't changed all that much.

Let's see how far he could push her. "You could drive over with me now and get acquainted with Hobo while I take a shower and clean up."

"Hobo? What kind of name is that for a female cat?"

"How was I to know she was a female? Gert clued me in, but I'd named her by then. Coming with me?"

She frowned—being in the same place with him while he showered wasn't such a good idea. Time to set things straight, Amy thought. "Ever since we first met I seem to hear you telling me the best way to get places. Since we've decided to be friends, I want to be up front with some things, one of them being that I do not like controlling men.''

He let out a bark of surprised laughter. "Me? Controlling?"

"You tend to take charge without consulting me. First you wouldn't let me drive to Tiny Tim's by myself, you had to show me in person. It didn't seem worth an argument so I let it go. Then you wouldn't tell me how to get to the hotel, even though I asked you to give me directions. You insisted on taking me there. Again I didn't protest because, well, actually I didn't expect to see you again."

David thought it over for a moment or two. "I see your point, but I think you're being a tad sensitive about what's meant to be controlling and what isn't. Try this on—maybe I was merely trying to be a gentleman."

"What about the fact you just asked if I was coming with you to your place to hang out while you showered?"

He shrugged. "You didn't say yes or no and I badly need a shower. I was trying to speed things up."

He could see she was considering that.

"I see your point, too," she said finally.

"That's what friends do—give each other a little slack when necessary." He waited to see how she'd react to that.

He thought her "True enough" was a bit forced. For some reason she was determined to stick to the idea of them being friends. Well, why not? He might be wary of any other type of involvement with a woman, but what was the harm in being friends with Amy?

"Compromise is also what friends do," she said. "So I'll follow you to your apartment to meet Hobo. That way you won't have to drive me back here."

She was one up on him there. Could be fun to have her for a friend.

"Sounds good," he told her, and gave her the address in case they got separated on the way.

Then he watched her walk away. She'd changed into jeans, and as he took note of her curvy bottom, he decided it might not be all that easy to be "just friends" with Amy Simon.

Chapter Three

At his apartment, David pointed out the cat to Amy and started for his bedroom to grab some clean clothes before he showered.

"Wait," Amy called after him. "Hobo and I need to be introduced by you."

He paused. "Why? She's a cat."

"She's your cat. And a very pretty tortoiseshell. Your introduction will let her know I'm okay."

He rolled his eyes but walked back and knelt down beside Amy, who was holding out her fingers for Hobo to sniff.

"Hobo," he said, "meet Amy. She's a friend." He rose and bolted for the bedroom before Amy could come up with another wacky idea.

He was back in ten minutes, showered and wearing clean jeans and T-shirt.

Amy was sitting on the floor petting the cat. "Where's her box?" she asked.

"Litter box?"

"No, I mean her birthing box. For her to have the kittens in."

"Gert didn't tell me she needed that."

"Hobo has to get used to the box ahead of time so she won't go off and have the kittens in the corner of a closet or a dresser drawer left open. Or even on your bed. I don't think you'd care for that since birthing is rather messy. You need to be prepared."

"I wasn't planning on becoming the father of kittens, you know."

"Obviously. Do you happen to have a fair-size cardboard box somewhere?"

He found one, as well as an old blanket for Amy to put in the bottom of the box and several old towels to cover it. She placed the box in an out-of-the-way corner of the living room. "Now, put Hobo in the box," she said. "She'll sniff all around in it and probably jump out, but she'll know it's there. You can keep putting her in it when you're home so she gets the idea it's hers."

"See what I got myself into for taking you in," he told the cat as he lifted her gently and set her down inside the box. "Special cat food bowls that won't tip over, water bowls that fill when you need a drink, kitty litter for the sandbox and now this."

"She doesn't seem to have any fleas," Amy said.

"Gert told me she wouldn't. Fleas don't like high desert—the elevation here is almost five thousand feet."

Hobo leaped out of the box, pausing to smell the outside of the cardboard, then she brushed against David's leg before going over to sniff at Amy's shoe. Amy bent and stroked her behind the ears, murmuring, "I'll be back to see you, pretty girl."

Which meant she planned to return to his apartment in the near future. Before he started picturing her in his bed, he reminded himself the key word was *friends,* not *lovers.* If he kept his hands off her, and he definitely meant to, maybe the chemistry he could still feel between them would lose its potency.

As Amy straightened, Hobo let out what could only be described as a mournful yowl. He stared at the cat. Was something wrong with her?

"Uh-oh." Amy plopped down beside Hobo again, this time gently feeling the cat's stomach. "I think you got that box ready in the nick of time. She's in labor. You'd better put her in it."

"You mean now?" David said, his blue eyes widening.

"Yes, right now."

He very gingerly lifted Hobo and carried her to the box. She sniffed it again and seemed to settle down to stay. He started to walk away, but the cat climbed out and followed him, yowling.

"She's one of those," Amy told him.

"Those what?"

"If you don't sit by the box while she has at least the first kitten, she'll keep following you and have the kittens wherever you are. Some cats are like that. Others demand total privacy."

"You mean I have to play vet midwife? I studied law, not medicine."

"She'll do all the work, but she's bonded with you and she needs the security of you being nearby."

David sighed, put Hobo back in the box and eased down on the floor next to it. "You're the cat expert," he told Amy. "How about joining me here?"

He knew Amy had chosen the corner so the cat could feel partly hidden, not for space, and this made for a very cozy situation when Amy sat next to him— she was practically in his lap. Such near intimacy made it difficult for him to keep the word *friend* in mind. She smelled faintly of some light floral scent he couldn't identify despite his recent acquaintance with nursery plants. Whatever it was, he liked it.

Keep your mind on the cat, Amy warned herself as her knee brushed against David's thigh. This chemistry thing is merely a matter of endorphins, nothing you can't ignore. But ignoring the feeling was darn hard when she was crowded against him.

Hobo began to growl, focusing her attention. The cat's ears went back as she crouched in the box, and suddenly a kitten's head pushed its way free of her. The rest of the kitten followed quickly and Hobo turned to the tiny thing and began licking it clean.

"Looks like a drowned mouse," David commented.

The next kitten was tinier than the first and Hobo nudged it away from her without trying to clean it, returning her attention to the firstborn.

"You need to put that reject under her nose so she'll have to take care of it," Amy said.

"I need to?"

"She trusts you. I'm still a stranger."

By the time David cautiously moved the rejected kitten closer, a third one was being born. Again Hobo pushed the second born aside to tend to the new one.

"Why won't she take care of it?" he asked.

"The poor little thing is the runt of the litter. Cats seem to sense that the smallest one has the least chance of survival, so they tend to the others first. The trouble is, the runt can die during this time."

"You mean the kitten may be defective?"

"It's a possibility."

David's expression changed from puzzled to determined as, muttering about handicaps, he persisted in setting the tiniest kitten in front of Hobo until she finally gave up and started washing the runt. By the time the fourth and last was born, the runt had revived enough to crawl to a nipple and join the other two.

"No matter if she is a runt," David said. "She deserves a chance."

Because he'd identified the kitten as female without any evidence, Amy decided his words might well pertain to more than the kitten, but she hesitated to pry. To help David, as she intended to do, she needed to gain his confidence before asking any personal questions.

"You gave her one," she told him.

"And she ran with it. A fighter. She'll do okay."

They both started to get up at the same time and collided in the narrow space. She grabbed him for balance and his arms went around her. Amy could feel the sizzle of heat as he held her close for a longer moment than either needed to regain their balance. As he released her, she gazed into his eyes and noticed how dilated his pupils were—a sure sign that touching her affected him. Hers probably were, too, since she could hardly deny she didn't want him to let her go.

"Uh," she said, backing away, "now you need to ease those messy towels out from under her and let her lie with the kittens on the clean blanket underneath. If you don't, she may try to move the kittens to another spot. It's an instinct to get rid of the birth odors so the kittens will be safe from predators."

He grunted but did as she said. Once he'd disposed of the towels and washed his hands, he said, "Care to celebrate the birth of Hobo's four kittens by having dinner with me?"

"I think you should stay with her for a while."

"They deliver pizza."

With the memory of him holding her still potent, she started to refuse. On second thought, though, eating pizza with him would actually be a casually friendly thing to do. "Pepperoni," she said.

"With sausage."

Lots of cholesterol, but she could afford that once in a while.

"Sounds good."

While they waited for the delivery, Amy decided to pursue her plan of covert therapy under the cover of comradeship. "What's there to do around here when you're not working?" she asked.

David took a while to answer. "You ever been up in a sailplane?" he asked finally.

"I don't even know what one is."

"You've heard of gliders." At her nod, he continued. "A sailplane is a sophisticated glider, designed aerodynamically to stay in the air as long as the pilot can find a thermal."

"You lost me somewhere along the way."

"You've seen hawks soaring up and up without moving their wings. That's because they're in a column of rising air—a thermal. Actually, it'd be easier to show you this weekend."

"You mean you have a sailplane?"

"Some play golf, I sailplane. Been doing it ever since I got my pilot's license ten years ago."

Somewhat reassured by the fact he'd been at it for ten years and so must be experienced, Amy still had a problem. "I'm not all that crazy about flying," she admitted.

"In commercial jets, you mean?"

Again she nodded.

"There's no comparison."

Maybe not, but was she prepared to do something she was sure would scare her just to further her acquaintance with David so she could help him with his denial problem?

He grinned at her. "Scared?"

She bristled. As a kid, the worst insult her older brother could throw at her was that she was a scaredy-cat. Just to prove to him she wasn't, she'd risked things in the past she shuddered to think of. Still, she wasn't a child anymore, so she shouldn't be swayed by David asking if she was scared. She might be, but she had no intention of telling him. Or backing down.

Raising her chin, she said, "Sounds like fun."

Later, as they ate the pizza, he told her more about sailplanes than she cared to know. Apparently lots of people flew them here in Nevada where thermals were frequent.

"It's so quiet up there, so beautiful," he said. "You feel like a hawk yourself, endlessly soaring."

"You've sold me," she said, realizing sailplaning was something he really loved to do. To join him might make her a trusted buddy, and she did need his trust if she was going to help him. Taking a deep breath, she added, "I'll give it a try."

Immediately after saying it, she rose from her chair at the kitchen table. "Time to leave." Yes, before she got talked into something else precarious. "I did enjoy the pizza, sausage and all."

He got up, too. "Thanks for the help with the kittens."

Which reminded her of how he'd assumed the runt was female. Why? Could be it really wasn't important, but she'd find out sooner or later. "Glad to be of service."

"I'll pick you up at Gert's Saturday morning around noon. Thermals usually form in the afternoon."

"You said you had a pilot's license. Do you have to be a pilot to fly sailplanes?"

"Yep. Have to learn about gliders, too."

"So I'm safe with you, I guess."

He was standing close to her. Too close. She ordered her feet to move away from him, but the order got garbled by what she saw in those deep blue eyes, and she remained motionless. He was looking at her like—like...

Without touching her otherwise, he bent his head and brushed his lips over hers. Every cell in her body yearned for him.

Safe with him? The words echoed in her head as she leaned into the kiss wanting more, needing more, even though she tried not to. Impossible not to relish the zing that ran bone-deep. *Good grief, all this without even being in his arms.* With a tremendous effort of will, she broke contact and literally fled from the apartment.

So much for being safe, she told herself as she climbed into her SUV. Clenching her teeth, she vowed to make sure that didn't happen again. *Friends* was the operative word—not *lovers.*

David found himself staring bemusedly at the door she'd closed behind her and forced himself into action. Clean up the kitchen. Take out the trash. Stop thinking about how soft and warm her lips were and how they'd yielded to his. Don't remember her taste or how she smells of flowers.

He shouldn't have kissed her. Been too long without a woman, Severin, he told himself. And this one definitely isn't a good choice for a quick affair. Very bad choice—your aunt's associate. Which was true, no doubt about it, but he didn't think it'd stop him from kissing her again, if the chance came.

On the other hand, she could be at loose ends, wanting no more than he wanted. Nothing even vaguely permanent. Just a test of how potent the chemistry was.

As he went into the living room to check on the kittens, he nodded. Start as friends, keep cool and see where it goes. Kneeling by the box, he stared down at Hobo and her brood of four, all fuzzy now as they nursed. The tiny one was completely black, the other three black and white. As he reached down and stroked the black one's head with a gentle finger, Hobo mewed.

"Don't worry, I'd never hurt her," he murmured. How could he, when the sight of that tiny body reminded him so much of Sarah, one and a half months premature and so small she'd looked like a doll, not a baby.

That had been five—no, six—years ago. He shared custody with Iris, his ex, but hadn't asked to have Sarah visit him since he'd left New Mexico last year. David sighed and got to his feet. Right now she was better off with her mother than him.

The next day, David pulled into Tourmaline's small airfield with Amy, parking near where his sailplane was tied down. She got out of his pickup and walked around the aircraft. "It's bigger than I thought it'd be," she told him.

"That good or bad news?"

She frowned. "Good, I guess."

He'd sensed her increasing nervousness as they'd driven to the field. "Aunt Gert's been up with me several times," he said in an effort to make her relax. "Grandfather, too."

"Your grandfather?"

"No, not mine."

"Well, he can't be your aunt's. She told me herself she's seventy."

"He's a friend of ours who goes by that name."

She stared at him. "You mean everyone calls him Grandfather?"

"He's a Paiute medicine man. Grandfather is a name of respect." David turned to greet a middle-aged man walking toward them. "Amy, this is Grant," he said. "Our tow pilot. Grant, my friend Amy."

Grant nodded to her. "Going up with this yahoo, are you?"

"I said I would."

"Can't renege on a promise, that it?" Grant chuckled. "Don't worry, I ain't crashed yet and neither's he."

"I'm not sure I like the sound of that 'yet,'" Amy told him.

"Safe as in your mother's arms. Notice I didn't say his arms." Grant nodded toward David, who was busy untying the sailplane. "I can recommend his flying, but the other's up in the air." He chuckled again before turning and walking toward a small red-and-white plane parked a ways in front of the sailplane.

"He's going to attach the towline." David lifted the top canopy of his plane and gestured toward the rear seat. "After you."

Amy climbed in and closed the seat belt around her. When he was satisfied the towline was secure, David climbed into the front cockpit and fastened down the canopy.

"It's an adventure," Amy muttered under her

breath, resisting the impulse to close her eyes as both planes began moving. When's the last time you had anything approaching an adventure? she asked herself. She'd been living, as Grant put it, safe as in her mother's arms, for so long she couldn't even remember feeling adventurous.

Which reminded her David's arms would hardly be safe. Another adventure she wasn't ready for?

Before she realized what was happening, they were airborne. Though she could hear the drone of the tow plane's motor drifting back to her, the noise level in the sailplane was nil. Nothing like taking off in one of the big commercial jets.

"I'll drop the tow at about three thousand feet." She could hear David clearly.

"How high will we go then?" she managed to ask after swallowing twice.

"As high as the thermal we find will take us. No higher than ten thousand feet, though, or we'd need oxygen."

"How do you know where the thermals are?"

"Search and find. Watch the birds. Get lucky."

As soon as David unhooked the towline, Grant's plane turned away from them and disappeared from her view. Now there was no sound at all as they drifted. She decided not to ask how they were going to get back down with no motor. Glide, she supposed, feeling her fingers begin to hurt from clenching her hands together so tightly.

"Okay back there?" David asked.

"Fine." She hoped she sounded more convinced than she felt. It wasn't so much that she questioned his expertise. For some reason she trusted him, knowing he wouldn't have asked her to join him unless he was sure it was safe. But the sailplane itself was new to her—how strange to be up in the air with no motor.

As if reading her thought, David said, "Think of the plane as if it was a sailboat. The boat in the water is driven by the wind in the sails, and up here our plane is driven by air currents under the wings."

Amy examined the idea and began to relax. "I've done a lot of sailing in Lake Huron and around Mackinac Island," she told him.

"Maybe you'll have a chance to show me sometime. I've sailed, but I'm more a flier than a sailor."

That just might be possible, since her brother's father-in-law had a sailboat docked at his Lake Tahoe condo in Incline Village and Tahoe wasn't all that far from Tourmaline. That is, if she and David managed to stay friends without going off the deep end—and she didn't mean the pier. That kiss last night...

"Thermal coming up," David said. "Here we go."

She braced herself, but nothing really happened except the sailplane began to climb, rising in wide circles, reminding her of how the red-tailed hawks soared above her brother's horse ranch in Carson Valley. She could see the peaks of the Sierras, some still snow-capped, in the distance. The lack of any noise did remind her of a sailboat, except on a boat things creaked. The plane itself didn't make a sound.

Peaceful, and the sky, oh, so beautiful, hardly a cloud in sight. This must be how it feels to be a bird, she thought, admitting that she was actually enjoying herself.

Up and up they soared, she couldn't believe how effortlessly. When, some time later, she realized the plane was descending, she sighed. "Does this mean we have to land?"

"The thermal's shifting away from the field. It's a long walk back if I don't keep the plane fairly close to the field, so we can glide down pretty much where we went up."

So she was right—they'd glide down. The thought didn't bother her now. David knew what to do, just as she knew how to tack a sailboat into port.

After they'd glided back to earth, tied the plane down and were once again in the pickup headed for Tourmaline, Amy said, "Thanks for the experience— it was fun. Awesome, even. I might even go up again if you ask me."

David glanced over at her and grinned. "Anytime." She'd been a good sport. His ex-wife had refused to go up with him before they were married, and didn't change her mind after she was his wife. Maybe that should have told him something. He understood now that Iris's idea of flying involved riding in privately owned jets. Like Murdock's.

"You ever been married?" he asked.

She blinked, obviously somewhat surprised at the abrupt change in subject. "No. If you want a reason, it's because I like being in charge of my life myself."

"As good a reason as any."

She opened her mouth as though to speak, glanced at him and closed it.

He shrugged. "I brought it up, so go ahead and ask me why I'm divorced."

"Gert sort of suggested you may have married the wrong woman."

He half smiled. "She was blunter than that when she met Iris before the wedding. 'Run and don't look back' was her advice to me."

"You know, that's almost exactly what I told my brother before he married his first wife. It was a disaster."

"Which may be why you and Gert are both shrinks."

"Your aunt never did marry, did she?"

"My mother told my sister and me Gert was engaged to an Air Force pilot in World War II who got shot down over Germany."

Amy sighed. "And she never got over him. How romantic."

He shot her a skeptical look. "I'm not saying my aunt never looked at another man. She just never married one."

"Makes her human, but it's still romantic. So you have a sister?"

"Diane. She's a teacher in Hawaii. Unmarried."

"Smart gal," Amy quipped.

"Where does your brother live?"

"Russ? He has a horse ranch near here, in Carson Valley. That's one of the reasons I answered your aunt's ad for an associate. I wanted to be closer to him and my nephew and baby niece."

David frowned. "He didn't learn the first time, I take it."

"Not all marriages are bad. Mari's a great gal. They suit each other like you wouldn't believe."

"So you do believe in marriage as an institution."

She nodded. "For some people. Not for me. I'm happier single."

"I agree with that philosophy. Totally."

"Ground rules for friends," Amy said.

"Wouldn't have it any other way."

"Maybe we ought to set a few others while we're at it."

He grinned at her. "Ones we can keep like the first rule or ones we can't?"

She shook her head at him. "You know what I mean."

"Yeah—fatal attraction."

"It's chemistry," she sputtered. "Hormones. Pheromones."

"All of the above. But how does that stop me from wanting to pull over and haul you into my arms right now?"

He watched her start to bristle, then deliberately take a deep breath before speaking. "If we're able to ignore it, the temptation will eventually fade." Her tone was cool.

That raised his eyebrows. "If you believe that, I don't know how you ever got to be a psychologist."

"I can do anything I make my mind up to do," she said coolly. "Including ignoring."

She'd just laid down a challenge. David smiled. He hadn't felt like taking up any challenges for more than a year, but he sure as hell meant to run with this one.

Chapter Four

As the week passed, Amy found she was having a hard time controlling her impulse to go outside and talk to David during her lunch break. By noon Friday she broke down and found him in the side yard, washing off with the hose.

"Just wondering how the kittens are doing," she said, trying not to be affected by all those water droplets glistening on his bare torso. Good grief, did she really feel an urge to lick them off one by one?

"Growing. Even Sheba."

Putting any crazy thought of temptation firmly aside, she decided to zero in on his conviction the runt was a female. "If you mean the little black one, how do you know it's a she?"

He shrugged.

"Well," she said, "I guess Sheba's no stranger

name for a male than Hobo for a female. Actually, if you look you can tell.''

''I did. They all look alike to me back there.''

''Female anatomy in kittens sort of resembles an exclamation point.''

''You could come over tonight and show me.''

Not to his apartment, not at night. Bad idea. ''How about tomorrow instead?''

''Whatever. Then we can—explore.'' His smile was devilish.

''The countryside, you mean?'' she said quickly. ''Okay, but not up quite so high this time.''

''That's what friends are for—to take you to the heights.''

''We've been there.'' She put a pinch of tartness in her tone.

''So now you expect the depths? How about Sutro's Tunnel? That's ground level and a tad below.''

''Never heard of it.''

''How about the V&T Railroad?''

She shook her head.

''Virginia City?''

''That I've heard about from my little nephew. He claims camels live in Virginia City.''

''He's right, but only during the annual camel races. The Virginia and Truckee Railroad still runs between Virginia City and Gold Hill. Want to take a ride on the rails with a genuine steam engine pulling the cars?''

She smiled. ''Why not? If I survived the sailplane, the V&T ought to be child's play.''

"There's a tunnel along the way, with an interesting tradition to go with it."

Analyzing the teasing light in his eyes, she said, "Maybe I don't want to follow tradition."

"Where's your when-in-Rome spirit?"

Left behind long ago, she almost told him. Along with my spirit of adventure. "I'll come by tomorrow about ten," she said. "That way you won't have to pick me up or drop me off. See you then."

She turned from his mocking gaze and returned to the house. He could make fun of her wanting her own transportation all he wanted to, but she was determined to play it safe. At least until this nearly irresistible urge to touch and be touched by him wore itself out from lack of fuel.

If she wanted to help David face his denial, she certainly couldn't afford to be caught up in a sizzling affair with him. Even if she wasn't trying to act as a covert therapist, getting intimate with the nephew of the psychiatrist who was monitoring her last six months of pre-licensure would be a mistake, to say the least. Besides, she had no intention of becoming involved with any man at this stage in her life. Maybe once she had that license in her hot little hands she'd feel differently. After all, what was wrong with having an affair with an eligible man if the circumstances were right?

"You look somber," Gert told her as she came into the office.

"I was thinking about David," Amy said truthfully. Under Gert's inquiring gaze, she had no choice but to go on. Since she certainly wasn't going to go into the chemistry between them, she came up with something that had been bothering her. "He seems straightforward and, well, honest."

"Which makes you wonder about the trouble he had in New Mexico over a year ago."

Amy nodded. "I realize it may be none of my business."

Gert glanced at her watch. "We'll discuss it after office hours."

Later, after the office had closed and the receptionist left, Gert suggested they enjoy some limeade on the front porch. "David's left for the day, so now we can talk," she said. "I doubt he'd care if I told you, but I'm sure he wouldn't care to overhear it being told.

"First of all, he was in one of those high-falutin' law firms in Albuquerque, not yet a full partner, but being groomed to be—though still low enough on the totem pole so he had to take cases none of the others wanted. This case was one of them. Before it came to trial, David began to suspect his wife, Iris, was having an affair. Anyway, the case itself doesn't matter. What does matter was that while it was being tried, one of the jurors claimed he was bribed."

"By David's law firm?"

"Not specifically, but the hint was there. Naturally the judge dismissed the jury and set a date for a new trial. The senior partner of the firm, Brent Murdock, seemed to support David, but that was an illusion. Murdock subsequently handed him his walking papers, offering a lot of false sympathy of the we-know-you're-innocent type, but for the sake of the firm's good reputation, you have to go. At the same time, Iris announced she was getting a divorce.''

"A double blow," Amy murmured. "Do you think David was set up?"

"Of course. Especially since, once the damage was done, the juror retracted his bribe accusation. Before David left Albuquerque, he got an anonymous letter claiming the writer had something on Murdock. David believed it was from the juror, but by then he was too dispirited to follow up on it. Who wouldn't be? With Murdock handling the divorce, even though he hadn't taken a divorce case in years, it was soon evident to David that he was the man Iris had been seeing on the sly.''

"It sounds so tawdry."

"Exactly. David went into law with high ideals, only to be betrayed by a man he respected and trusted—Murdock. It led to disillusionment with the law itself. I believe what Murdock did to him was far more traumatic than Iris's betrayal. As far as she's concerned, my feeling is good riddance. A shallow woman, interested only in herself.

"In any case, David went into a depression which he refused to have treated. It's taken him over a year to recover.''

"Do you think he really has come back all the way?" Amy asked. "He's still refusing to consider returning to law.''

Gert sighed. "I think he misses Sarah, too.''

Amy blinked. Iris was the ex-wife. Who was Sarah?

"She's his six-year-old daughter," Gert continued.

"A shy child, but smart. She was a preemie and has a limp the orthopedists say can't be surgically fixed."

The runt who might be handicapped. No wonder he'd insisted the black kitten was a female. "Does his ex-wife have custody?" Amy asked.

"It's joint. David had enough fight left to insist on that. He's paying child support, but he hasn't once asked to have Sarah come here to visit."

So David hadn't faced up to his responsibility for his daughter's emotional health, either. Divorce was tough on kids. Sarah might even be wondering if he'd left because of something she did.

Amy could see there was a lot of work ahead of her in her undercover plan to treat David. She wished she could talk to Gert about it, but there was the possibility Gert would order her to cease and desist. Then she'd have to.

"I'm glad you and David recovered from your temporary misunderstanding," Gert said. "I was hoping you'd be friends."

"I think we're beginning to be," Amy told her. No more than the truth, if one ignored the underlying problem of sexual attraction.

Was it possible that they could solve that by getting it out of their systems? She shook her head. Too risky. What if lovemaking merely accelerated the need?

Amy spent the next morning before ten looking for an apartment, not wanting to burden Gert any longer than necessary. She found two possibilities, but neither would be available for a month. When David let her into his place at ten, she told him what she'd seen.

"Why don't you move into this complex?" he asked. "The guy above me is moving out tomorrow. I don't think they've rented it yet. How much are they asking for the places you saw?"

She told him, and it turned out the rent was less in his complex. Since money was a consideration, she upgraded her instinctive answer from "no way" to "better think about it." After all, living in the same complex as David didn't mean she was moving in with him.

Hobo seemed to recognize her scent when Amy put her hand into the box for the cat to smell, because she made no fuss when Amy picked up the kittens one by one and looked at their tiny behinds. "Two girls, two boys," she told David after the kittens were once more nestled against their mother. "And you did guess right with Sheba. Have you named the others yet?"

"She's the only one I plan to keep—along with Hobo. I'll let the new owners of the other three name them."

"Don't tell me you've already found people to take the kittens," she asked as they stood up and moved away from the kittens.

"If they don't back out. As Grandpa Severin used to say, 'There's many a slip twixt the cup and the lip.' Not to mention the other slipups along the way."

"I learned fairly late that life wasn't fair," Amy said. "It's a chastising experience at any age. You were lucky, though, to know your grandfather. A lot of us don't get to."

"I'm his namesake." David smiled. "We were what he called 'good buddies' when I was young."

"Was he a lawyer, too? Gert said your father was."

"No, he raised cattle. I was sure I was going to be a cowboy when I was a kid."

"Do you occasionally wish today that you'd been able to be?"

David frowned at what sounded to him like a shrink question. After living with his aunt for those two months before he found this apartment, he could spot one a mile away. Still, Amy was also a shrink, so she probably couldn't help thinking that way. "No."

"Really? Not even a smidgen?"

"Before I reached my teens I had a cowboy period, a fireman period and a cop period. None really stuck with me."

"Except law?"

Another shrink question. He glanced at her, trying to decide if she was just making conversation, oblivious to how she sounded, and found her looking at him expectantly, her lips slightly parted. Which made him forget all about questions.

Holding her gaze, he took a step toward her. How green her eyes were, like the ocean, wide and deep enough to drown in. Her pupils dilated and for a moment she didn't move. He was close enough to touch her before she started backing away.

"I—uh—weren't we going to Virginia City?" she stammered, as she dodged around him and headed for the door.

She insisted it was her turn to drive. It was pure

luck they met Tom, the apartment manager, on the way to her SUV. David introduced them, and mentioned the soon-to-be-vacant apartment.

"If you've seen David's, you know what it looks like," Tom told her. "I haven't rented it yet, got to clean the rugs and paint the place first. Won't take long. With David here to vouch for you, if you want it, let me know by Tuesday, okay?"

Amy agreed she'd let Tom know, and they walked on to her SUV. Though unsure whether it was a good idea to have her living that close, David knew he wanted her to take the place.

"Never driven one of these," he said when they reached the vehicle.

"Do you really want to try or is this some macho ploy to put you behind the wheel instead of me so you won't have to let a woman drive?" she asked.

"Whoa, Doctor. I thought it was an innocent observation, but you shrinks analyze everything so how do I know what you thought I meant?"

Amy bit her lip. "Sorry."

"I'm easy—you can drive. I doubt it'll seriously disturb my masculinity."

"I guess I'm still reacting to that phony persona you tried to lay on me before we sorted out who each other was."

They got in and he grinned at her. "Cal's a great guy. You might like him."

"Cal?"

"Yeah, I borrowed his persona, as you call it— dogs, beer, the works. Might have overdone it a tad." To get rid of you before the fire started, he didn't add.

"A tad?"

"So I'm a ham actor."

On the drive up to Virginia City they traded names of actors and movies for worst performances of all time.

As she parked the SUV near the V&T depot on a back street in the town, Amy said, "To be fair, sometimes old movies just seem awful because the mores of the years they were filmed in were so different from today's. Take smoking—in old movies everyone seems to be lighting a cigarette, taking a drag or putting one out."

"Cal may drink beer, but he doesn't smoke," David said.

"I think I've heard enough about Cal."

"Someday I'll introduce you."

She slanted him a look. "Who knows, I may like him better than you."

When they reached the depot, the locomotive was just pulling into the station. They bought tickets and joined the other passengers waiting to board the open cars.

"How long is this trip to Gold Hill?" she asked.

"About two miles around the curves and through the tunnel."

"The tunnel with a tradition?"

"You got it. Once the V&T was the richest—and the 'crookedest'—railroad in the country. This is all that's left of it."

"Crooked as in winding or as in nefarious?"

"Could be both—most railroad magnates got rich quick."

The conductor called "All aboard," and the train huffed away from the station toward Gold Hill— downhill all the way.

When they approached the tunnel, David glanced at Amy. From her don't-touch-me expression he knew she expected the tradition involved a kiss. That might have been his original intention, but, since he'd made up the tradition for the tunnel in the first place, he had the right to change it.

When the train plunged into sudden darkness, he reached for her hand and held it in his, brushing his thumb lightly over hers. Her hand soft and warm in his made him want more, like touching her in any way did.

When the car burst into sunlight again he let go. She raised her eyebrows at him. "That's it?"

"The meaning's what's important. You know the area is full of gold and silver mines, active in the old days. If two members of the opposite sex held hands in that tunnel, it meant a bonanza was ahead for them both. If they failed to do this, they faced a *borrasca*."

Not bad, he thought, for a spur-of-the-moment tradition.

"I know *bonanza* means *good luck,* but what's a *borrasca?*" Amy asked suspiciously.

"Another Mexican word meaning just the opposite. Bad luck, a disaster. They're both mining terms."

"That's a rather romantic tradition."

He nodded, trying not to look smug.

At Gold Hill they got off and walked around what was almost a ghost town, then reboarded the train for the uphill ride back to Virginia City. At the tunnel, he felt her reach for his hand, and a spurt of pure delight washed over him as their palms met and he felt her thumb brush his in a subtle caress. Bonanza, right enough, even though she did let go when the tunnel ended.

After they left the train in Virginia City, they walked up the steep hill to the main street and wandered along the quaint wooden sidewalks past the preserved old buildings now housing museums, casinos and gift shops, stopped for ice cream cones and continued on to a bench, where they sat while finishing the cones.

"I've been thinking about your accusation," Amy said. "You're right. My questions have been, well, you might say probing."

"I did say."

"Sometimes it's hard to remember which hat I'm wearing."

"Just a plain sunbonnet is good enough for me."

She stared at him. "Why a sunbonnet?"

"Sun's warm and we're steeped in history up here. A sunbonnet would put you in character."

She shrugged. After throwing the paper from her finished cone in the trash barrel next to the bench, she said, "Anyway, to be fair, I've decided it's your turn to ask me probing questions if you want."

"Let's see." While he thought, he noticed her lift her chin and sit a little straighter, obviously bracing herself, so he decided to come in obliquely and surprise her again. "Why are your eyes so green?"

After a moment, she smiled at him. "That's an easy one. I inherited the Simon green eyes from my great-grandfather. We all have them. The rest of me is courtesy of my great-grandmother's genes. I look a lot like her. Great-Grandpa shocked the rather proper New England Simon clan by falling in love with a Broadway chorus girl and marrying her. He founded the Michigan Simons, a somewhat less stiff-necked branch.''

He stared at her and blurted, "I dreamed—" He broke off one word too late. Damn.

"You can't leave me hanging."

"My motto is never tell a shrink any dream."

"But I'm your friend, not your shrink."

He figured she wouldn't let him off the hook until he told her. What the hell, cleaned up a tad, the dream wasn't revealing. "The first night after I met you I dreamed you were on stage in a chorus line and I was watching you from the audience. Think your great-grandma was responsible?"

"Who knows? It's strange you happened to hit on something like that in your dream."

"Yeah." He had no intention of telling her the rest of the dream. Just recalling it drove him partway up. "Ready to go on?"

"Walking or with asking probing questions?"

"Either."

"I've given you your chance, so I'll opt for walking."

They left the bench and, eventually, the wooden sidewalk, then followed the road until they finally came to the entrance of an old cemetery, one that was clearly no longer used as a burial ground. No visitors strolled between the graves.

As they entered, Amy said, "I'm used to big, shady trees in cemeteries. This looks so stark."

"When the mines were in operation, every last tree for something like a hundred miles in every direction was cut down for fuel or for mine timbers. For years nobody replanted trees up here."

"Nevada has its own kind of beauty, though. I love the mountains."

"We've got our share."

"You talk like a Nevadan. Do you plan to stay in Tourmaline?"

He might be unduly sensitive, but wasn't she verging on probing again? "As opposed to where?" he asked.

"The rest of the world." Tartness tinged her words, making him smile.

"Haven't made up my mind." He pointed. "There's a semishady cottonwood by that iron fence over there."

On the way over to the tree, she paused to read a nearly obliterated inscription on a tilted stone. "'He shot me once. Once was enough for E. Nuffe.' Do you suppose the victim actually composed this epitaph?"

"Depends on how long the lead poisoning took to be fatal."

She frowned at him. "Very funny."

When they stood under the shade of the cottonwood, David pulled her into his arms and kissed her, her lips soft and responsive under his. She tasted like a sweet combination of maple-nut ice cream and of herself. He breathed in the faint scent of flowers.

Aroused by the feel of her against him, he deepened the kiss, his mind gradually shutting down, over-whelmed by the passion gripping him. Who was he trying to fool? There'd been a time last year when he hadn't felt any need for a woman, but, hell, in the past he'd never needed any woman with such desperate intensity as he needed Amy right now. She lit a fire that nothing short of having her would quench.

Amy clung to David, unable to think, pressing closer, wanting more of him, all of him, refusing to hear the tiny part of her that warned she was being unwise. Since when had a kiss turned her liquid with need? She doubted any other kiss had ever triggered the wave of passion engulfing her. The time, the location, the world all vanished. David held her, nothing else existed. Every moment since she'd met him had been leading up to this one. He made her crazy.

If she could melt into him, become a part of him, she would. His scent, uniquely David, surrounded her, his taste, tinged with mint from his ice cream was pure David. His name throbbed through her with every heartbeat.

His mouth left hers to trail kisses to her ear, where he whispered, ''If we don't stop, we'll wind up making love right here in the dirt.''

The tiny rational core of her mind knew that was a bad idea no matter how much she wanted him at the moment, dirt or no dirt. His words brought her far enough out of her daze to understand they had to call a halt before it was too late. With a deep sigh, she released David. He held her for a long moment and then let her go.

"Close call." The rasp of passion blurred his words.

She wanted to respond, to agree, but what was there to say? They'd come together like iron filings and a magnet. Irresistibly. *And would do it again, given the chance,* her inner voice reminded her.

"I suppose we should talk about it, but what's the use?" she said finally.

He half smiled. "Never thought I'd hear a shrink admit talking it out wouldn't help."

"It's—it's irrational. On my part, at least. You're a male and therefore—"

"Stop right there. What just happened to us had nothing to do with my testosterone level. It's been simmering between us ever since you walked up to me at Aunt Gert's."

The truth, plain and simple. She may as well admit it. "Then we'll have to take steps to see it doesn't come to a boil again."

He raised an eyebrow. "Got any ideas how?"

Ideas? With him standing no more than a foot away looking at her with those searing blue eyes, she could hardly think at all. What she really wanted was to be back in his arms, even though she knew better.

"What color are your eyes, anyway?" she demanded.

He blinked. "My driver's license says blue."

She scowled at him. "I mean what color blue?"

"Never thought about it. What's that have to do with my wanting to haul you back in my arms and kiss you senseless?"

"More than you think. The exact shade of your

eyes and what to do about this—this unreasonable attraction are both questions I can't find an answer to.'' She turned away from him, putting temptation behind her, and began walking toward town.

He followed her. As they reached the wooden sidewalk, he said, ''Still friends?''

''We're certainly not enemies.'' She heard the tartness in her voice with a smidgen of dismay. It wouldn't be wise to start blaming David when they were both guilty. Lust was a perfectly normal human condition, not wrong if two people harmed no one by giving into it.

The problem for her was that she'd decided to be his secret shrink. How in the world could she accomplish that if they became involved in an affair? Since she wasn't officially his therapist, though, and he had no notion she was even his covert one, it actually wasn't a professional therapist-patient association where sexual involvement of any kind was an emphatic no-no.

Still, she felt she had to give up one thing or the other. Should she forget trying to help him, even though she believed he was in denial about the past, and plunge headlong into an affair, or should she retreat to a precarious friendship and try to help him? How could she ever reach a decision?

''Hungry?'' he asked. ''The food's not bad in there.''

She glanced around, saw they were walking past an old-time casino called the Bucket of Blood and shook her head. ''Not yet. The cone filled me up.''

She meant to stop there, but more words spilled out. "You tasted minty."

"And you tasted like maple-nut." He grinned at her, took her hand and, holding it, swung their joined hands between them as they continued along the wooden sidewalk.

Unaccountably, her spirits lifted. She might not have made a decision, but that could wait until tomorrow. She and David still had the rest of the day to spend together and she was going to do her best to enjoy it. Who knows, maybe by some miracle they could manage to be just friends.

Her inner voice whispered *Yeah, and maybe you'll look up tomorrow and see turtles flying in the thermals with the hawks.*

Chapter Five

David spent Sunday, Monday and Tuesday trying to
convince himself he didn't want to get entangled with
any woman, no matter how hot he was for Amy. Apparently she felt the same because he didn't catch so
much as a glimpse of her while he worked in Aunt
Gert's yard.

On Wednesday morning, when he parked his
pickup in front of his aunt's place, she hailed him
from the front porch. "Amy tells me she's moving to
your apartment complex this weekend. I hope you're
planning to help her with the move."

News to him that she'd called Tom and agreed to
take the apartment. He'd figured she might back out.
"Amy hasn't asked me," he said.

"Don't be an idiot. Of course not. She probably

has some peculiar notion about not bothering you. You need to offer.''

He shrugged. ''Okay, tell her I've offered.''

Aunt Gert gave him an approving nod. ''Plan to have breakfast here with us at nine on Saturday.''

''Thanks, I will.''

There wasn't a sign of Amy all that day. When he got home that evening, he found a manila envelope in the mail with no return address and an Albuquerque postmark. Inside was a page clipped from the Albuquerque *Journal* with a write-up of Iris Fenton and Brent Murdock's June wedding—an elaborate affair, Iris in a white bridal gown, Murdock in a tux. An unsigned note tucked in with it had ''So what about this?'' scrawled across it in what David felt almost sure was the same handwriting as the anonymous note he'd gotten before he left New Mexico.

It didn't surprise him Murdock had married Iris. His ex-wife was a past master—or was it mistress?—at getting exactly what she wanted, never mind running roughshod over the bystanders. Something like Murdock. The two deserved each other.

Instead of tossing the whole thing in the trash, David put the note and clipping back in the envelope and placed it in the same folder as the anonymous New Mexico note. He checked the handwriting against the first note and saw many similarities. As he put the folder away he told himself if he ever needed to try to trace the note, he'd look up that juror first. In the meantime he'd keep both notes safe.

The clipping upset him, bringing back the bad days in New Mexico. Aunt Gert believed it was depression that drove him to Nevada, but what actually had made him leave was he'd been afraid he'd lose control and kill Murdock. Easy enough to do with the old Texas Colt his grandfather had left him along with the legacy.

Gradually he became aware of Hobo brushing against his legs, mewing plaintively, and he realized she needed to be fed. He focused his mind on the cat, saying, "Mothering's a hungry job, right?"

While she was tucking into her food, he had a look at the kittens. All but the runt had their milky-blue eyes open. He cradled Sheba in the palm of his hand for a moment. "Don't worry," he told her. "You'll catch up."

Amy had told him unless they had some Siamese genes in their ancestry, their eyes would change color, to green or yellow. He tried to keep his mind from drifting back to the past, but holding the runt had reminded him of Sarah. What must she think, his poor little daughter, her father gone and her mother married to a stranger? He didn't give a damn about Murdock being Iris's husband, but it grated on him to think of the bastard taking his place as Sarah's new father. He was still brooding about it when the phone rang.

"Hi," Amy said. "Thanks for your offer to help me move on Saturday. I've got some boxes and things in the back of the SUV that I can't carry alone, so I really do appreciate it."

"No problem."

"How're the kittens?"

He told her.

"Well, guess I'll see you Saturday, then," Amy said. "Thanks again."

He hung up, smiling. With Amy moving into his complex, anything might happen. And probably would, given their incendiary attraction.

The woman who cooked for Gert didn't work weekends, so Amy helped make the pancake breakfast Saturday morning. David arrived in time to fry the bacon he insisted had to go with the pancakes.

"There's going to be a powwow at the reservation in July," Gert told them as they ate. "I told Grandfather we'd all be there." She glanced at Amy. "I made the assumption you'd be interested. Forgive me if I was wrong."

"You were right," Amy said. "I've never been to a powwow. Or met a genuine Native American medicine man. I'm looking forward to it."

"Good. He's looking forward to meeting you, too."

Amy stared at Gert. "Me?"

"I called him last night and mentioned that I thought you were the second hawk, the female he dreamed about, so naturally he's interested."

At a loss, Amy echoed, "The second hawk?"

"He says David is the male hawk," Gert answered.

Bewildered, Amy said, "I don't think I understand."

"You'll have to wait until you meet Grandfather. It goes beyond the scope of science, but I've come to believe that he does have prophetic dreams."

"He doesn't even know me."

"Makes no difference," David said. "Grandfather is no ordinary man."

"So you'll be coming to the powwow, too," Gert said.

"Wouldn't miss it," David told her.

When they finished eating, Amy started to help clean up, but Gert shooed her away. "You've got your own tasks to attend to today. I'll just putter around here while you and David make the move. I know you want to be on your own, so would I in the same circumstances, but I'll miss having you living here in the house. And, David, while Amy's getting settled in, come back and pick up the things from the attic I've set aside for her to use."

"Describe the 'things,'" David said. "I need to know if it'll be a one-man or two-man job."

"It's merely a bed, a dresser and some odds and ends," Gert said.

"Two-man."

"How about one man and one woman?" Amy asked. "I'm perfectly capable of helping."

David gave her an assessing glance, then said, "Here's my take. We'll load the smaller attic odds and ends into the pickup and, on my way back here, I'll stop and see if Cal can help out for a half hour with the heavier ones."

"Our Cal from Tourmaline Nursery?" Amy asked.

"The one and only."

She raised her eyebrows. "Whatever."

Once they'd hauled the pickup load into her new apartment and he'd helped Amy carry up the boxes she'd had in her SUV, David got back in his truck and stopped at the nursery.

"Cal's not here," Max Conners, the owner, told him. "You must not have heard what happened. He was coming to work on his Harley last Monday and some hockey puck in a van sideswiped him."

"How bad is he hurt?"

"Busted some bones. The worst is, the jerks in the van—two passengers and the driver—say Cal cut in front of them, so it's his fault. One witness told the cops different, but then she changed her story to say she doesn't know what happened. Cal thinks she got threatened by the van guys. It's a bitch of a world, that's what I say."

David nodded. "Is Cal still in the hospital?"

"Naw, these days they don't keep you any time at all. He's home, his mom's helping him. Lucky for me school's out—I got his kid brother filling in here."

"Got his phone number handy?"

After Max gave him Cal's number, David drove back to his aunt's. She was sitting on the porch with a husky teen-age boy David recognized as the kid who lived next door.

"Randy's going to help you move the heavy stuff," Gert said. "I heard about Cal. At least he'll be all right, poor thing."

It didn't take long to load the bed and dresser in the truck nor to unload and carry them up the stairs to Amy's new apartment, after which David slipped Randy a couple of bucks and drove him back home. When he returned to the complex, Amy was taking the last few items from her SUV.

"Since that was Randy, what happened to Cal?" she asked.

"Bad news." David went on to tell her about Cal.

"Bummer. What are you going to do about it?"

He stared at her. How in hell had she figured out so quickly that he intended to do anything?

"I know you're going to help him," she added. "Lucky for Cal he has a friend who's a lawyer."

He knew he'd probably have to resort to law, but the first thing on the agenda was to talk to Cal and get the name of the witness who changed her story. The all-too-familiar scenario left a bitter taste in his mouth.

"Maybe I can help," Amy said. "I figure you'll probably interview the witness. Since she's a woman, it might help if I went with you. Sometimes women talk easier to other women than to men."

He found himself annoyed that she'd jumped into what wasn't even a case yet before he'd so much as contacted Cal. Since she was right about women talking more freely to other women than to men, he let it go. He might need her.

"Gert sent over some limeade and cookies," Amy told him. "Come on up to the apartment and we'll have some while we discuss the case."

"It's not a case."

"But it will be."

"Stop right there. I don't know if Cal wants me to do anything, so there's nothing to discuss."

Amy bit her lip. "Sorry. It's your field, not mine. I got so excited about the possibility you'd be getting involved in law again, facing your bogeyman, so to speak, that I trespassed.''

David felt as stunned as if she'd whacked him over the head with a psychology textbook. Facing his bogeyman? It might not be a shrink phrase, but what she'd just said was certainly a shrink attitude. ''Who appointed you my therapist?'' he demanded. ''If Gert sicced you on me, I swear—''

''No, no, your aunt didn't ask me to do anything. And of course I'm not your therapist. It's just that I can't help seeing that you're in denial about the past. It's possible—''

His hand sliced the air between them. ''Enough! No more jargon. No more analyzing me. Understand?''

''I hear you, but—''

His annoyance sliding into anger, David was about to turn and walk away when he heard a familiar voice.

''Oh, Brent,'' a woman said. ''There's David, over by that SUV.''

He didn't have to look around to know it was Iris, beyond a doubt. She was damn brave to turn up here with that bastard in tow. He swung around.

''Daddy?'' Sarah's plaintive voice cooled his rising rage. He looked at her instead of at the other two, six-year-old Sarah staring at him as though he were a stranger.

He strode over, crouched in front of her and held out his arms. She hesitated, but then came to him and he held her tight for a long moment. When he let Sarah go and rose, he kept hold of her hand while he waited to hear what Iris wanted now. She always wanted something.

She was, he noticed, sleeker and more expensively dressed. She glanced at Amy and frowned. "Perhaps we could go to your apartment, David."

"Here is fine." He wasn't giving an inch.

Iris shrugged. "If you insist. Sarah has come to pay you a visit while Brent and I take our delayed honeymoon cruise." She laid a crimson finger-nailed hand on Murdock's arm and smiled up at him.

Murdock hadn't spoken yet. Now he nodded, murmured something that might have been a greeting, then said, "We'll be gone at least three months."

So they were dropping Sarah off with him with no warning, almost as though she were a pet rather than a child. With an effort he forced himself to shut off his anger at the two adults and concentrated on his daughter.

Looking down at her, he told her the truth. "I've missed you, punkin. I'm happy you're here, happy you'll be staying with me for a while."

Sarah offered him a shy smile, clinging to his hand as though to a safety line. She didn't once look at her mother or at Murdock.

"That's settled, then," Iris said briskly. "We left Sarah's things with your aunt. Kiss Mommy goodbye, dear." She bent and offered her cheek. Sarah kept hold of David's hand while she gave Iris's cheek a quick peck.

"Now say goodbye to Daddy Brent."

Sarah mumbled something unintelligible, her grip tightening on David's hand.

Daddy Brent. The words made David want to gag.

"Well, then we're off." Iris's bright smile didn't reach her eyes. Holding Murdock's arm, she walked toward the white Mercedes parked across the lot, her heels clicking on the blacktop.

"Sarah, my name is Amy." The words brought David's awareness back to her.

"Amy's my friend," he told Sarah, which wasn't quite a lie. He couldn't really call her an enemy just because she'd tried to practice her profession on him without his knowledge or consent. To give her the benefit of the doubt, she might not have realized what she was doing until he brought her up short.

"Your great-aunt Gert made us some limeade and cookies," Amy told Sarah. "Why don't the three of us go up to my new apartment and share them?"

Sarah looked at David, who smiled at her. "I know I'm thirsty," he said, "and it's very good limeade."

"Do you live there, too?" Sarah asked him.

"I live in another apartment in this complex."

"Your father's cat has kittens," Amy said. "After we finish our snack I'm sure he'll take you over to see them."

Sarah's blue gaze settled on David. "Kittens? Really? How many?"

"Four."

"Mommy won't let me have a kitten 'cause she doesn't like cats," Sarah confided as they climbed the steps to Amy's apartment. "*He* had a dog, but Mommy made him give it away 'cause it smelled, she said. It sort of did but the dog liked me, I could tell."

David found himself elated when she referred to

Murdock simply as "he." Obviously she didn't think of him as Daddy Brent.

"You like animals, don't you?" Amy said.

Sarah nodded.

In Amy's apartment, Sarah finally let go of his hand to climb up onto a stool at the kitchen counter. She sipped at the glass of limeade Amy handed her, looking down at the glass, rather than at either of them.

David had mentioned his daughter had a limp, Amy thought, but it wasn't noticeable. Possibly because she wore what looked like orthopedic shoes. One could have a lift inside. Her eyes were the same gorgeous blue as David's. Except for her momentary animation over the kittens, Sarah seemed quite shy. A quiet child often was a child with problems.

"Have a cookie," David said, pushing the basket of cookies toward Sarah. When she hesitated, he added, "It's okay."

She took one, nibbling at it.

"If you like, you can take the cookie with you," Amy said, certain that the little girl must be eager to see the kittens.

David drained his glass, grabbed another cookie and slid off his stool. "Let's go, sweetheart."

He glanced at Amy and she could see his indecision, see him weighing the odds—should he ask her to join them or not? She figured he wouldn't. For one thing he was peeved with her and for another, he must want to get reacquainted with his daughter.

"Want to come?" he asked, surprising her.

"Just for a moment to see the kittens," she told him.

She stayed long enough to watch Sarah drop to her knees beside the box, her face rapt as she gazed at cat and kittens.

"Your father named two of them," Amy said to her. "Hobo's the mother and Sheba is the tiny black one."

David took Sarah's hand and held it close to Hobo's nose for the cat to sniff. "This is Sarah," he said. "She's my daughter and your friend." He let go of Sarah, reached into the box and picked up the black kitten. "Hold out your hands," he told Sarah.

When she did, he deposited the kitten onto her palms. "Look," he said, "Sheba's eyes are beginning to open. Kittens keep them closed for a week or so after they're born."

Sarah studied the kitten intently. "Just a little open," she said at last. "Do you think she likes me?"

David glanced at Amy as if for help, so she answered. "Sheba's too small to know about liking yet, but I'm sure she feels safe with you holding her because you're so very careful."

"I like her," Sarah said. "I like her best of all."

"That's good," David told her, "because Sheba is going to be your kitten." He lifted Sheba as he spoke and eased her down next to her mother. "Right now she needs to eat like her brothers and sister."

Sarah stared at her father, awestruck. "I get to have my own kitten?"

"You sure do. After all, I have my own cat."

Sarah digested this, finally smiling broadly.

Amy knew an exit cue when she saw one. "See you guys later," she told them. "Welcome to Tourmaline, Sarah."

After the door closed behind Amy, Sarah turned to her father. "Do you think Amy likes me?"

What was all this business about worrying whether animals or people liked her? he wondered. He didn't recall his daughter being so unsure of herself before.

"I'm willing to bet she does."

"She's nice."

"Yes, she is," he said absently, troubled about Sarah. Had he ever in his life told her he loved her? He was ashamed that he couldn't remember. Unable to get the words out now, he tousled her hair. "I'm sure glad you're with me in Tourmaline, punkin," he told her.

She giggled. "You used to call me that before."

"And you used to tell me you weren't a pumpkin, that pumpkins were round and orange."

Her pleased grin was his reward for remembering.

"You never met your great-aunt Gert," he said. "We'll be going over there in a bit to get your belongings."

"I'm going to stay here with you?"

"You sure are." He tended to use the second bedroom for storage, but it did have a single bed in it. "I didn't know you were coming or I would've fixed your room up better. Just as well, this way we can do that together."

"Mommy says Great-aunt Gert is a psychiatrist." Sarah pronounced the difficult word precisely, as though she'd been drilled in saying it.

"Right. Do you know what that means?"

"*He* didn't think I heard him, but he said she takes care of crazies."

David managed to conceal his spurt of anger. "Psychiatrists are doctors who help people who have problems," he told her.

"Maybe she won't like me."

"Hey, kid, she'll love you. Trust me." Now he found he could say it. "I love you and she will, too."

Her expression showed such doubt it made his heart ache. Why shouldn't the poor kid doubt him? He hadn't so much as written her a letter in over an entire year, much less made any effort to see her.

He could apologize, but what would that mean to a six-year-old? What he had to do was gain back her trust. Somehow.

At Gert's he had to coax Sarah out of the truck, and she clung fiercely to his hand as they walked up to the back door. Gert must have seen him pull into the drive because she had the door open before they got there.

"Hello, Sarah," she said. "Welcome to Tourmaline."

Sarah gaped at her. "Amy said that."

Gert smiled. "We both say welcome to people we like."

"You do?"

After nodding, Gert invited them inside. "Would you like to shake hands with me, Sarah?" she asked.

After some hesitation, Sarah released David's hand and held hers out.

"There, now we're introduced," Gert told her, "and we can start learning how to be friends."

After grasping his hand again, Sarah said, "Daddy introduced me to Hobo."

"Good for him. Cats make great friends."

"And he said Sheba is my very own kitten."

Gert glanced at David. "Every little girl needs a kitten."

"We'll visit longer another time," he said. "Right now I need to borrow some single sheets if you have any, plus pick up Sarah's stuff."

"I have some stored in the cedar chest. How about a quilt to go with them?"

"Great."

While Gert went to get the sheets, David found Sarah's belongings in the hallway leading to the front of the house. With Sarah clinging to his hand, he had to stack the two suitcases, one under his arm, holding the other by the handle. Sarah insisted on trotting out to the truck with him while he loaded them in. He couldn't blame her for feeling insecure—her life had been radically changed in the last year.

Back in the house with Sarah, he collected the sheets and quilt from Gert.

"You don't keep any of them in your house, do you?" Sarah asked suddenly.

"Keep what here, dear?" Gert asked.

"Crazies, like *he* said."

"Murdock," David muttered, damning the man.

"No, I do not," Gert said. "You needn't worry about that. Sometime, when we know each other better, we'll talk about what I do. All right?"

Sarah nodded dubiously.

When they were driving back to the apartment, Sarah said, "Great-aunt Gert's sheets smell nice."

"That's from the cedar in the chest where she stores them." He wanted to discuss the "crazies" business, but decided to leave that up to Gert. How had she known exactly the right thing to tell Sarah when they went in, that saying welcome to someone meant you liked them? He shrugged. Obvious. Gert was a shrink, after all.

"She said she liked me," Sarah told him, as if reading his thought.

"Pretty soon you'll run out of fingers to count all the animals and people who like you, punkin."

Sarah giggled. "I'm not a pumpkin."

He wanted to pull over and hug her, to never let her go, to keep her safe always. Instead he said, "You're not? From where I sit, you look pretty round and orange to me."

"Oh, Daddy, you're so silly," she told him, still giggling.

Her words warmed his heart.

Chapter Six

David didn't sleep well that night, mostly because he feared Sarah would wake in a strange room and be frightened. But she slept soundly. By morning, he decided he needed help to make certain he didn't do anything that might upset his daughter. He knew he couldn't ask his aunt, because Sarah was her grand-niece and there was a rule about it being unethical for shrinks to treat relatives. Even though he didn't want Sarah treated, exactly, just advice about what he should or shouldn't be doing, he was sure Gert would refer him to someone else. Who?

Amy. Right. She wasn't a relative and Sarah seemed to like her. He was over his irritation at Amy, convinced she hadn't deliberately tried to analyze him. He'd set her straight about never doing it again, even involuntarily. She must realize now that, whether it suited her or not, the way he was suited him. Sarah was a different story. For one thing, she needed to gain more self-confidence.

He couldn't call Amy since her phone hookup wouldn't be in till Monday. Glancing at his watch, he decided she might not be up yet. As he made coffee, he pictured her lying asleep in the bed he'd assembled yesterday. If he knocked on her door right now and woke her, would she answer the door in whatever she wore to sleep in?

Hobo came into the kitchen and wound around his ankles, breaking his reverie in the nick of time. Much more and he'd have been at her door trying to find out. He was feeding the cat when Sarah appeared, rubbing her eyes, reminding him he wasn't exactly free to act on impulse.

"I looked at Sheba, but she was sleeping all curled up with the others," she said. "So I didn't pick her up." Her uncertain expression told him she was waiting for approval.

He nodded. "Kittens need a lot of sleep. Want to help decide what we'll have for breakfast?"

Before she could answer, the doorbell rang. He opened the door to Amy, who entered carrying a basket covered with a napkin.

"Hi, David and Sarah," she said, lifting the napkin. "I made some blueberry muffins."

"Hi, Amy," Sarah murmured.

David drew in the mouthwatering scent and smiled. "Can't recall when I last had muffins for breakfast. Sit down and join Sarah and me."

"I don't want to intrude."

"Hey, you made the muffins, you get to eat them with us. Right, punkin?"

Sarah nodded. "Only I'm supposed to get dressed first."

"School's out, right?" Without waiting for an answer, he went on. "This is vacation time so we get to lounge around in our nightclothes if we want."

"You're dressed," Sarah pointed out.

"That's because I'm a man and we're entertaining a lady. Since you're a lady, too, you can wear your pj's in front of her."

Sarah glanced from him to Amy and back, finally saying, "Okay." She climbed onto a counter stool.

Thanks to Gert's reminder to stop for milk yesterday, Sarah had a mug of milk while he and Amy had coffee. He realized there were going to be other things he'd need to be reminded about. Lots of others. When it came to six-year-old girls, he knew next to nothing.

When they finished eating, Amy said to Sarah, "Do you take a bath at night or in the morning?"

Sarah lowered her head. "At night, only I forgot last night."

She meant her father forgot to ask, David thought.

"So you can take it this morning for once," Amy said. "No harm done. Do you run the water yourself?"

Sarah nodded but looked hesitant.

"Since you've never used this bathtub before, why don't I go in with you?" Amy said. "You probably won't need help, but just in case."

The relief on his daughter's face was obvious as they left the kitchen.

David cleaned up their dishes while they were gone. After about ten minutes, Amy came back to the kitchen alone. "Sarah's in the tub," she told him. "She's quite capable for her age, but terribly unsure of herself."

"I've noticed." David cleared his throat. "I've been wondering if you'd sort of help me with her. I don't mean therapy, just to tell me the right things to do."

Amy eyed him. "The first thing is to establish a good relationship with Sarah. You two need to spend quality time together, whether it's going places or simply hanging out together."

He frowned. "I can handle taking her places, but what places? And how the hell am I supposed to know how to hang out with a six-year-old girl?"

"You once were six."

"Yeah, but I was a boy."

"You were a child at six and so is she. What did you like to do then?"

David thought back. "When we visited my grandfather, I got to ride a pony. That was my cowboy period."

"A pony's no problem. I think I mentioned my brother has a horse ranch just up the road in Carson Valley. My nephew has a pony Sarah can ride. Also, I saw a Camel Rides sign while I was driving to Tourmaline. I bet you never got to ride a camel."

"I bet you never did, either," he countered.

"Right, but it's a possibility for Sarah. She'd be safe enough if you held her."

"You want me to ride a camel?" His voice was tinged with disbelief.

"Why not?"

"Hey, you thought it up, you have to come, too. We could go this afternoon."

Amy blinked. "Well, I—"

"Scared?"

She shot him a dirty look. "No more than you. Seriously, though, you and Sarah need to do things together, just the two of you."

"Okay, we will during the week. This is Sunday and so the three of us can ride camels together."

She sighed. "I suppose I'll have to."

"That's the spirit. Right now I have a favor to ask of you. I called Cal last night and I'm going over to talk to him this morning. Would you stay with Sarah while I'm gone? I shouldn't be more than an hour at the most. I was going to leave her with Gert, but Sarah's—" He paused, the word *stepfather* refusing to come out. "Sarah overheard the man her mother is married to say that Gert took care of crazies and so she's still a tad dubious about Gert. She'll be more comfortable with you."

"No problem, but do you mind if I bring her over to my place?"

"Fine with me. I'll pick her up there when I get back and we can decide what time to ride those camels."

After David left, Amy helped Sarah decide what she wanted to wear, letting her know they were going to ride camels later.

"Real camels?" Sarah asked, wide-eyed.

Assured they were, Sarah chose jeans and a T-shirt. "My daddy's coming with us?" she asked as she got dressed.

"He's going to ride on your camel with you. Right now, we're going to make your bed and then you can come over to my apartment until your father gets back. He'll pick you up there."

"Mommy says now that we live in the new place with *him,* it's the maid's job to make the beds."

"Your father doesn't have a maid, so here it'll be up to you to make your own."

While they were pulling up the bedcovers, she noticed Sarah push something under the pillow. From the glimpse she caught, it looked to be a stuffed animal so well-loved as to be scruffy. It was too early in their relationship to ask about it, so she didn't comment. As it turned out, Sarah did have a fair idea of how to make a bed.

"Very good," Amy told her. "I can see you'll be a real help to your father."

She got a dubious look. "I will?"

Amy nodded.

Later, with Sarah over at her own place, Amy expanded on that comment. Sitting on the couch with the little girl, she said, "Your mother is who taught you about taking baths and brushing your teeth and when to change out of dirty clothes, things like that. Your father's been gone for a while so he's forgotten about those things, and you'll have to tell him. That's part of what I meant about helping him."

Sarah nodded solemnly.

"Now, I'd really appreciate it if you help me sort through a box of odds and ends I'm trying to unpack and we can decide where they'd look the best in my new apartment."

Hesitant at first, Sarah soon warmed to putting knickknacks around and changing them from place to place. When the box was empty, Amy offered her a black-and-white wooden cat with an extra-long tail, something she'd seen the girl admiring.

"This is for you," she said, "not only because you're a good helper, but because I like you."

"To keep?" Sarah asked.

"Yes. It's a present."

Sarah held the small figure as carefully as she'd handled the live kitten, staring down at it. After a moment, she looked up at Amy almost, but not quite, fearfully. "I forgot to say thank you."

"No, you didn't, you just said it. Do you know almost every language has words for *thank-you?*" Amy proceeded to go through French, Spanish, Russian and German thank-yous.

When she finished, she encouraged Sarah to try saying the words. "When your father helps you with something, you can tell him thank-you in German and then he'll probably say, 'When I wasn't looking someone changed my American girl into a German.'"

Sarah giggled. "That's silly." Almost immediately she looked stricken.

"It's okay to be silly sometimes and to make people laugh," Amy assured her.

After a long silence, Sarah asked, "Can you say *pumpkin* in those other languages?"

Remembering how David had called her punkin, Amy realized this might be important to Sarah. "You can, I'm sure, but I don't know the words. I have a French dictionary somewhere around here, though, so we can look up the French word."

Fifteen minutes later, Amy and Sarah were chanting *"citrouille"* together, over and over. By the time David returned, Sarah had it down pat. He walked in to find them both giggling.

"What so funny?" he asked.

Sarah looked at Amy, who said, "It's a surprise, so we can't tell."

"It's a surprise," Sarah echoed. "For you."

"I like funny surprises," he told her. "Right now it's time for you to meet Tiny Tim. We can pick up subs and drinks for lunch there, put them in a cooler, and picnic somewhere along the Carson River after the camel rides."

"I don't know how to ride a camel," Sarah said.

"Neither do I, neither does Amy, but we'll find out together."

Amy wondered what, if anything, the talk with Cal had produced, but she knew better than to ask. This was Sarah's day. Besides, she'd come close to shattering David's trust in her with her offer to help him with Cal's case. She had to be more careful.

"I still have some of Gert's cookies for dessert," she said.

"Will I like Tiny Tim?" Sarah asked.

"You won't see much of him," Amy told her, "but I bet you'll like his sandwiches."

After a stop at the café, they pulled onto the highway, Sarah sharing the back of the pickup's dual cab with the cooler. "I never rode in one of these before," she said.

"Two firsts so far today, then," David said, "with one more to come. Your first time in Tiny Tim's, your first ride in a pickup and soon your first ride on a camel."

"I bet Tim isn't very tiny," she said. "I could only see his head, but it looked big."

"Tim's over six feet and built like a bear," David confirmed.

"Sometimes people get nicknames that are just the opposite of what they look or act like," Amy said. "Like calling him Tiny."

Sarah didn't say anything for a long time. "That's mean," she finally said.

"Tim doesn't mind," David said, "or he wouldn't have named his café Tiny Tim's."

"But nicknames can be mean," Amy added, "if the person making up the name does it to hurt."

Sarah said nothing more until they arrived at the camel rides. When they got out she grasped her father's hand, and when they walked over near the camels, she reached for Amy's hand as well, staring up at the tall beasts. One turned its head and looked directly at them.

"What long eyelashes," Amy exclaimed.

"In their home desert, those lashes help keep their eyes safe during sandstorms," the man standing near the camels said. "If you want rides, the little girl will have to be held by Mom or Dad."

Mom or dad? Amy realized then they must look

like a family, and the thought gave her a pang. If she never married, would she ever have a child of her own? She believed children were better off with a male and a female parent, so she wasn't planning to be a single mother. On the other hand, she wasn't planning to marry, either.

The guy's words jolted David. Dad, yes, but Mom was off on her honeymoon with a cold-blooded traitor. He glanced at Amy and decided she'd be a better mother than Iris could ever imagine being. Too bad Sarah wasn't her daughter. "Dad'll take her with him," he told the man.

Sarah's tight grip on his hand told him she was scared. "It's okay," he murmured. "You're with me." His own words made him realize he'd do anything in the world to keep his little girl safe.

Two of the camels knelt down. After being instructed what to hold on to, and what to expect, David was helped onto one by the camel man, who then handed him Sarah.

He found he wasn't sitting on a saddle exactly, or if it was a camel saddle, it was nothing like what went on a horse. He held Sarah securely with one arm, using the other hand to grip the projection on the front. When the camel rose to its feet, he felt himself slide forward, then was shoved backward. With a side-to-side swaying gait, his mount walked placidly behind the man leading it. Too much of this, he thought, and a guy could get seasick.

"Are you scared, Daddy?" his daughter asked him in a near whisper.

"Not much. Are you?"

"A little bit. It's way high up."

He risked a glance behind and saw Amy aboard a second camel led by a teenage boy. "Okay back there?" David called.

"I can't believe this was my idea," she told him.

He chuckled. "Amy's sort of scared, too," he said to Sarah.

When the ride was over and the camel knelt for him to slide off, he heaved a sigh of relief, and imagined Amy and Sarah were glad it was over, too.

"Daddy," Sarah said, once they were on the ground again, "when I get old enough I'm going to ride a camel all by myself, just like Amy."

What about just like good old dad? He shrugged. So she admired Amy, nothing wrong with that. He did, too, if differently. He tried to visualize Iris on a camel and shook his head. No way.

Amy joined them, saying, "We made it."

"A triumph of bravado over sense," he muttered.

She made a face at him.

"They sort of smell," Sarah said, "but I got used to it."

Both adults laughed.

Later, they found a county park that bordered the Carson River and laid claim to a picnic bench. When they finished eating, Sarah got to throw the remnants of the subs to the wild ducks swimming in the river.

"Look, they like me," she said.

"Do you know why?" Amy asked her.

Sarah shook her head.

"Think about what you're doing."

"I'm giving them bread."

"Yes, you're feeding them. What do you think will happen when you run out of bread?"

"They'll get mad at me." Sarah's voice was sad.

"Not exactly. They're hungry so they'll look for food somewhere else, yes, but it has nothing to do with you and everything to do with ducks. That's how ducks are. They don't like people, they like the food people throw to them. So don't be upset when they swim away."

When the bread and the ducks were gone, the three of them walked back toward the truck. "We'll stop and say hello to your great-aunt Gert on the way back," David said once they were in the pickup.

"She said she didn't have crazies in her house?" Sarah made it sound like a question.

"You know how when you get sick sometimes you have to go to the doctor and then you get better?" Amy asked her.

Sarah nodded.

"Sometimes people's bodies don't get sick, but their mind does, so that they can't think quite right. Your great-aunt is the kind of doctor who takes care of people's minds instead of their bodies. When people's bodies get really sick, they have to go to a hospital to get better. It's the same with people's minds. If their minds get really sick, they go to hospitals that take care of minds. So your great-aunt doesn't have anybody sick in her house with her."

"Oh."

"I work with her," Amy continued, "taking care of people with troubled minds. I lived in her house until I found my apartment, so I know your great-aunt as a friend. She's a nice person.''

"She said she liked me."

"Well, she's certainly not a duck you're feeding, so you can believe she really does.''

David saw Sarah looking at him as though for confirmation. With some effort he put his annoyance at Murdock for causing this problem aside. Choosing his words carefully, he said, "Sometimes grown-ups say things they shouldn't. Calling people with troubled minds crazies is like giving them a mean nickname.''

"Kenny calls me Speedy 'cause I can't run fast,'' Sarah said, looking away from them. "He makes fun of me all the time.''

What kind of nasty brat would pick on a girl with a limp? Whoever Kenny was, David wanted to kill him.

"Kenny's a boy in your class at school?'' Amy asked. At Sarah's nod, she added, "Kenny's what's called a bully. He thinks the kids don't like him so he picks on everyone.''

"He's mean.''

"That's because he has a troubled mind and no one is helping him to get over it.''

David well knew Amy's explanation was right, but he still had an urge to shake the stuffing out of the kid.

"I still don't like him,'' Sarah muttered.

"Why should you?'' Amy countered. "It's very difficult to like those who pick on us.''

"Mommy says I should like everyone.''

"Did you tell her about Kenny?'' David asked.

"No."

David glanced at Amy. What the hell was he supposed to say now?

Amy gave him a little nod and said to Sarah, "If your mother knew about Kenny she might feel differently."

Let off the hook, David decided there was a lot to be said for having a psychology expert aboard. Especially one who was a chorus girl lookalike.

At Gert's house, they found her sitting on the front porch.

"We've all had a camel ride," David said.

"I've never had the courage," Gert said. "Come sit here on the glider with me, Sarah, and tell me how the ride went."

Somewhat reluctantly Sarah obeyed. "I had to ride with my daddy," she said.

"Because he was too scared to ride alone?" Gert asked.

The little girl looked directly at Gert for the first time, saw her smile and seemed to relax. "We were both kind of scared," she admitted.

Gert reached for a box on the low table alongside the glider, opened it and handed the box to Sarah. "I thought you might like these to play with."

Sara began removing tiny cups and saucers. "I don't have any doll dishes," she said. After a moment, she added, "Thank you."

Gert turned to David. "There's a doll buggy in the attic you might want to bring down for Sarah. And, Amy, you remember the twin baby dolls I had on the dresser in your room? Why don't you fetch them.

Sarah and I will lay out the doll dishes to have all
ready for the twins. Then they can take a nap in the
buggy.''

David's glance at his daughter showed him she was
engrossed with the tiny dishes, so he left her with his
aunt and followed Amy into the house.

When he came down the attic steps with the buggy,
he heard tinkling music coming from a bedroom and
noticed Amy inside. ''Can't find the dolls?'' he asked.

''They're here, but I remembered the ballerina music box on the chest of drawers. Look at the cute little
ballerina going round and round. Don't you think
Sarah would love this?''

Leaving the buggy in the hall, David entered the
bedroom, coming to stand beside Amy. ''She ought
to like it,'' he agreed.

He was close enough to breathe in her faint scent
of flowers, one he was rapidly becoming addicted to.
It was dangerous to start anything with a bed so close
by, but he couldn't resist. Taking her arm, he urged
her into a turn. When she was facing him, he bent
and kissed her, her lips warm and responsive under
his.

As always, her taste, her softness against him sent
him spinning, losing control. Because he couldn't
help it, he let the spin continue, holding her closer,
savoring her nearness. He wanted more, but he
grasped the frayed ends of his control, forcing himself
to do no more than deepen the kiss.

Her lips parted to let him in, an invitation he wel-
comed, a prelude to consummation of a different kind.

Which they weren't going to reach today, not now and not here.

Still, he couldn't let her go. Never before had a kiss taken him so far so fast. He found her irresistible, and from the way she snuggled closer, he could tell she wanted him, too.

It would happen, he'd make it happen. He'd gone far beyond the notion that one session of sex with Amy would be enough, to wondering if he'd ever have enough.

Amy pulled back slightly. "We can't," she said, the huskiness in her voice betraying her need.

Slowly, reluctantly, he let her go.

Chapter Seven

David had a place picked out to take Sarah every day the following week. Wednesday it was the local library, and it turned out to be a successful excursion because, as it turned out, Sarah loved to read. It bothered him that he'd paid so little attention to his daughter in past years that he didn't even know what she liked to do.

Never again would he allow himself to become so involved in his work that family came second. What had it gained him? Betrayal by a man he'd trusted and the end of his marriage. He doubted if the marriage ever could have succeeded, given that he and Iris had so little in common—nothing really except Sarah. But he could have been more of a father.

Wednesday evening he and Sarah were sharing a pizza at home when Amy came to the door.

"No, thanks," she said when he invited her to eat with them. "I stopped and had Chinese. I came over to bring you this from your great-aunt, Sarah. She thought you might like it." Amy held out the ballerina music box.

So she'd remembered to ask Gert about it. He'd forgotten.

When Sarah didn't reach to take the gift, Amy placed the music box on the table and wound it up. The tinkling tune reminded him of holding Amy in his arms at Gert's.

Sarah stared, saying nothing as the tiny ballerina danced around and around. Suddenly she burst into tears and bolted from the kitchen.

David jumped to his feet, started after her, then hesitated. He had no notion what triggered her outburst—Amy might be better qualified to find out. In any case, tears undid him.

"Do you want me to go after her?" she asked.

He nodded.

He toyed with a slice of pizza, his appetite gone, while he waited. And waited. He was pacing around the kitchen when at last he heard water running and realized Amy must have persuaded Sarah to take her nightly bath. Finally Amy returned.

"How is she?" he asked.

"She's taken the duck and the submarine she said you bought her yesterday into the tub with her. She told me she chose the submarine and you the duck because you thought every kid needed a yellow duck in the bathtub. I think she'll be okay now."

"What in hell upset her like that?"

"The ballerina. It's my fault, I goofed. I didn't think about her limp. Do you realize Sarah's dream was to be a ballerina? She clung to it until the last doctor she was taken to said bluntly, in her hearing, that no surgery could correct the shorter leg."

David's chest constricted with the pain he felt for his daughter.

"I'm so sorry," Amy told him. "I wouldn't've hurt her for the world."

"It's not your fault. How could you know? I didn't even know."

"It's true no one knew—Sarah said she'd never told anyone. Another thing came out. She hates what she calls her 'ugly' shoes, the orthopedic ones she has to wear to make up for the shorter leg. I took a look at the one with the lift and I think someone who works with such things could put something similar in a good pair of sandals or sneakers so she'd feel more like the other kids."

"I wish she'd said something to me."

"Sarah keeps a lot to herself. In a way, it's just as well I goofed about the ballerina, because she let some of what's bothering her come out. She may be more open from now on."

"I'm going to find something unusual she can enjoy doing," David said. "I'm not sure what, but I'll find it."

Amy smiled at him. "An excellent idea. It'll build up her self-esteem." She reached for the ballerina music box. "I'll take this back to Gert."

As she turned toward the door, David stopped her and gave her a heartfelt hug. "I take back all my nasty cracks about shrinks,'' he said as he let her go. ''You're really helping me with Sarah.''

''I'm very fond of her. She's a resourceful and intelligent child who loves her father more than you may realize.''

David blinked against the sting of tears. He'd done little to deserve it, but Sarah loved him, anyway. He took a deep breath and let it out slowly.

''Sarah keeps asking when you can come with us again,'' he said. ''Gert says there's a children's museum in Carson City with hands-on stuff for kids. How about going there with us on Saturday?''

''I'd like to. See you then.''

David smiled as he closed the door behind her. He was as interested in having Amy along as Sarah was, and not just because she helped him understand his daughter better. Amy was good company. More than that. If he didn't make love to her soon, he'd be a basket case.

The children's museum turned out to be a good place for kids, as Gert had predicted, Amy thought as she, Sarah and David wandered from one exhibit to another. The kids could touch almost everything there, which made it much more interesting to them. Looking at her watch, Amy saw the Music for Children event was about to begin so she guided the other two toward the room where it was being held.

Unsure what to expect, Amy was pleased to find that after the demonstration, the kids were going to actually be able to hold and try to play small-size instruments. Sarah watched with some interest as the man and woman running the event played notes on a clarinet, a flute, a trumpet, a xylophone, a guitar and, lastly, a violin.

David reached over Sarah's head to touch Amy's shoulder when the violinist began, pointing at his daughter, who stared raptly at the woman as she coaxed sweetness from the strings with her bow. When the time came for the kids to hold the small instruments, Amy was amazed at how correctly Sarah placed the violin under her chin and how carefully she drew the bow across the strings.

"Can I learn to play this?" she asked her father.

"If I can find someone to teach you, you can," he said.

As it turned out, the woman running the event, Nell Archer, was beginning a Suzuki class in violin for children four to seven. "After that, they need a larger instrument than the miniature," Nell said. "If any of the children in the class show definite musical talent and wish to go on, I can arrange for private lessons."

David signed Sarah up for the class, which was beginning in Gardnerville, not too far from Tourmaline, in a week.

"That should allow you enough time to purchase or lease an instrument," Nell said, and gave him the name of a music store in Reno that handled the small violins. "Be sure and let your child chose the instrument herself," she added. "It's important she establish a rapport with her instrument even before she learns to play it."

"What's *rapport* mean?" Sarah asked Nell, surprising both Amy and David because she didn't usually speak to strangers.

Nell smiled. "*Rapport* means that you feel a certain violin call to you. Not out loud, of course, but here, in your heart." She put her hand on her chest. "It means that violin wants to be yours and the two of you will become close friends."

Wide-eyed, Sarah looked from Nell to her father.

"Ms. Archer is the expert when it comes to violins," he told Sarah.

Amy smiled inwardly. A perfect answer. David probably thought rapport with an inanimate object was as unlikely as she did, but he hadn't let his skepticism show. He might need to learn a few things yet, but he was a natural father.

After they left the museum, Sarah said, "Can we go find my violin right now, Daddy?"

David smiled and said, "As long as we're this close to Reno, we might as well do it today."

Sarah was beside herself with excitement on the drive there, but when they parked in the music store lot, she quieted down and, by the time they went inside, looked frightened. "What if none of the violins want to be my friend?" she asked in a small voice.

"One of them will. Just wait and see." David sounded so positive that Sarah perked up a bit.

The salesman, an older man, led them to the children's section of the store and patiently handed Sarah one violin after another, telling her to hold each under her chin to see how it fit. There were seven in all and Sarah had begun to look worried by the time he handed her the sixth. As she fitted it under her chin her eyes widened.

"Daddy, I can feel it," she cried. "This is my violin."

Completely outfitted with not only the violin, but a bow, a case, resin and extra strings, Sarah insisted on carrying the cased instrument herself. After putting her and the case in the back cab, David whispered to Amy, "Do you suppose Nell isn't a flake, after all?"

Amy shrugged. "Since I never played an instrument in my life, how do I know?"

"Me, neither, but I have to admit I feel close to my grandpa's old Colt .45. Rapport, do you suppose?"

She poked him with her elbow. "What is it with men and guns?"

Instead of answering, he ran a finger along her spine, saying, "Then there's you and me. Rapport like you wouldn't believe."

"I am not an inanimate object," she told him.

He grinned at her. "I suspected as much."

Since the lessons began on a Saturday, Amy came with Sarah and David for the first one, held at a grammar school in Gardnerville. Nell Archer greeted them pleasantly, but when the time came for the lessons to begin, she announced that having parents present distracted the children. All the adults were dismissed and the door shut behind them.

"I guess I'm just as glad," one of the mothers said to Amy. "I'd be more nervous than Betty."

"She's your daughter?" Amy asked.

The woman nodded. "I'm Cary McBride. Betty's the one with red hair and freckles. What's your daughter's name?"

Before Amy could explain, David spoke up. "She's Sarah—brown hair and blue eyes."

"Actually I think she and Betty are seated next to each other. Do you live in town?"

"Tourmaline," David told her.

"Really? How wonderful. So do we. Could we exchange phone numbers? Maybe the girls can practice together sometimes. I used to play the violin myself and I know practice is sometimes a drag alone."

"Sounds like a winner." David took the pen and notepad Amy handed him from her purse, scribbling his number on a sheet and handing it to Cary before taking hers down.

Cary thanked him, then glanced at her watch. "Do you think I have enough time to grocery shop here before the class is over? I'm way behind with everything."

"Go ahead," Amy said. "If it takes longer than you think, we'll tell Betty where you are and keep an eye on her while we all wait in the schoolyard."

"Thanks. I appreciate it." Cary hurried off.

Amy's first thought had been "harried mother," but on second thought, there might be more going on than that. Cary had been visibly tense.

"Practice," David said. "That means I have to listen to a beginning violinist—right?"

Amy nodded. "Maybe even two at a time."

He winced.

They wandered out to the schoolyard and Amy sat

on a swing. David eased in back of her, said, "Hang on," and began to push the swing.

As she gradually rose higher and higher, she called to him, "I have an old picture of my great-grandmother being pushed in a swing on a Broadway stage. I guess it was romantically risqué in those days."

"If you were wearing a short, flared skirt, it might be the same today," he called back.

"Dreamer."

After a time he said, "Going to let the old cat die," and sat on the swing next to her.

"I never heard that one," Amy told him as the arcs of her swing grew less and less.

"Courtesy of my grandfather. He always said that when he stopped pushing the swing I was in."

"In your cowboy era."

"Right. Which reminds me—what did you want to be when you grew up?"

She struck a dramatic pose. "The world's greatest actress, what else?"

"Then what?"

She sighed. "My father wanted me to be a lawyer, like he was. Like my brother was before he defected."

"You're not one, though."

"I started out to be, but..." Her words trailed off. She wasn't ready to tell him or anyone what had happened to her in college.

"So you defected like your brother. Is he the one with the horse ranch?"

She nodded. "Russ is doing what he always wanted to do."

"Good for him."

"We all should be working at what we want to do."

"Are you?"

Amy nodded. "I realized I wanted to help people with their problems." Which was part of the truth. When she'd dropped out of pre-law, she'd already decided drama wasn't for her. She'd chosen a psych major mostly because she'd hoped learning more about the mind would help *her*. Wanting to help others came later.

Should she ask David if he was doing what he wanted to do? Better not, he'd gotten touchy about that kind of question from her. She'd lay off for a while.

"Ever come close to getting married?" he asked.

"Not really." It wasn't a lie. After all, Vince had certainly never considered marrying her even if she'd once believed differently. Marriage to him would have been more of a disaster than what had happened. "And I'm not sorry," she added, a bit more emphatically than she meant to.

"You've met Iris," David said.

He obviously intended to let the statement speak for itself.

"Yes." She hadn't liked the woman, but she wasn't going to say anything negative about Sarah's mother.

"Even if she hadn't taken up with that bastard we couldn't have made a go of it," he said.

That had been clear to Amy from the moment she met the woman, but she kept her words neutral. "People often go into marriages with unrealistic expectations."

"Yeah. I'm cured. Once bitten, twice shy."

"Grandpa again?"

David nodded.

Though she wanted to point out what might apply to a marriage didn't necessarily apply to his profession, she kept her mouth shut.

After a silence, she said, "I asked Gert about a place that you might take Sarah to see about shoes other than 'ugly' ones. She called an orthopedist she knew and he gave her the name of a guy in Carson City who does that sort of thing. I'll give you the phone number and address when we get back."

"Thanks, I'll get on it next week."

"Which reminds me. My brother invited me to bring you and Sarah out to his ranch next Saturday. I told him that was the powwow date so he upped it to the following Saturday. Sarah will get to ride a pony."

"Nice of him. Let's plan on it. I'd like to meet this lawyer who defected."

Not long after the hour was up they went inside the school. The door to the room was open and it sounded as though all ten violin students were talking at once.

As they entered the room Amy saw that the red-haired girl who must be Betty was chattering to Sarah as both girls placed their violins back in the cases.

"Hi, Betty," Amy said. "Your mother went shopping for groceries. I told her you'd be with us on the playground until she got back.''

''Awesome,'' Betty said. ''Sarah and I'll get to hang out longer.''

Sarah looked happy at the prospect, which meant she liked Betty.

Outside, violin cases placed out of the way, the two girls grabbed swings. David pushed Sarah and Amy pushed Betty until Cary McBride came rushing up.

''I'm so sorry I'm late,'' she said. ''It took longer than I thought.''

''No problem,'' David told her. ''The girls enjoyed the extra time together.''

''I'm so glad.'' She glanced at her watch. ''Hurry up, Betty, you know we have to get home before your father does.''

Betty obeyed with no dawdling. That, combined with the note of strain in Cary's voice, made Amy wonder if the father might be a petty tyrant.

''Bye,'' Sarah called after her.

''See you next week,'' Betty called back.

''I really like her,'' Sarah confided as she climbed into the back cab of the truck. ''She's fun.''

Amy took note that Sarah didn't ask if they thought Betty liked her. Bless that little redhead for her exuberant friendliness. A few friends like Betty would do wonders for the girl.

''I'm cooking dinner tonight for you both,'' she told David and Sarah once they were on the road. ''I asked Gert, but she's busy.''

''What have we done to deserve it?'' David asked.

''Nothing. You're my friends, that's all.''

"I'll bring wine," he said.

"I think I like Great-aunt Gert, too," Sarah said. "She tells awesome stories."

"See, I told you," David said. "Counting Sheba, you've already used up all the fingers on one hand."

Amy understood he must be referring to those Sarah liked—or maybe those who liked Sarah. Or both.

Dinner was a success despite the fact Amy forgot the potatoes and they almost burned. Afterward, Sarah drifted into the living room because she'd been promised she could watch the newest Disney movie on the VCR. David started it for her, then went back to help Amy with the cleanup.

The dishwasher took care of almost everything so they were soon finished. "We could go watch the movie with Sarah," she suggested.

"If I sit on a couch with you," he told her, "watching a Disney movie will be the furthest thing from my mind. How about sitting out on the balcony?"

Since each second-floor apartment had a tiny balcony off the living room, the balconies weren't exactly private. Which was just as well, Amy decided, remembering all too clearly what a struggle she'd had pulling herself away from David when he kissed her in the bedroom last week at Gert's.

Private or not, they had no sooner walked through the sliding door onto the balcony before he pulled her into his arms. "Long time between kisses," he murmured as he covered her mouth with his.

Every time he kissed her, she melted, there was no

help for it. Never before had any man's kiss made the world blur and then vanish. Never before had her entire being responded to the touch of a man's lips. Only with David.

There could be only one resolution to how he made her feel. Somehow, though, it never seemed to be the right time or the right place to make love. The knowledge that this night and this balcony was neither didn't prevent her from pressing closer, clinging to him while he held her tight against him, her softness pressed against his hardness.

"We fit," he whispered against her lips.

The sound she made in agreement was somewhere between a moan and a purr. How had she let herself get into such a state? One touch and she felt like a sparkler, sizzling and shimmering all over. What had happened to her boast to herself that no man could ever make her lose control? They hadn't even gotten naked yet and she was so far gone that if he threw her down on the cement floor of the balcony all she'd do was encourage him.

When finally they drew apart, she had to lean against the railing to steady herself.

"We'll drive us both crazy if we go on like this much longer," he rasped.

"I know."

It wasn't as simple as her going to his apartment after Sarah was asleep and sharing his bed. What if Sarah woke up? No matter how much she wanted to make love with him, she'd never do anything that might upset Sarah. And, of course, he couldn't come to her apartment and leave Sarah alone in his, even if she was asleep.

"I've heard anticipation is half the fun," she said, trying to inject a lighter tone.

"To hell with anticipation. I want you now."

The growl in his voice settled deep into her bones, setting up vibrations that threatened to undo her. He must know how much she wanted him, too. Now.

A picture flashed into her mind—some comic, was it Carol Burnett?—ripping open her dress and leaping onto the lap of a startled man crying, "Take me, I'm yours!"

Imagining herself doing the same thing, Amy began to giggle.

"What's so funny?"

Between giggles, she tried to tell him.

The end result was a hard kiss, one that left her breathless, then a swat on her butt, sending her toward the door. "Disney it is," he said ruefully.

Chapter Eight

The following Saturday, a beautiful high desert July day, hot and dry, Gert insisted David drive her car to the Pyramid Lake Paiute reservation, saying, "I may be agile for seventy, but it's hard to look graceful hauling myself up into that pickup of yours. Sarah and I will sit comfortably in back, thank you."

Which left Amy in the front seat with David, which suited him just fine. Once they were under way, he heard Sarah ask Gert, "Are you really seventy years old?"

"And holding," Gert told her.

"*He* said smart people retire at sixty." By now they all knew that "he" meant her stepfather. "I know what *retire* means, because I asked my teacher," Sarah continued. "My daddy said you were a really smart lady, but you told me you still take care of people with troubled minds and that means you're not retired.''

"Actually I did retire at sixty-two," Gert said. "They had a party for me at the hospital in Las Vegas where I worked and I made a speech about how old psychiatrists never die, they just shrink away. Then I moved to my retirement home in Tourmaline and pretty soon I was bored because I had nothing to do that interested me. So I decided to try to take care of just a few people. A few became a lot. I needed someone to help me and I found Amy."

"That was lucky."

Sarah didn't know how lucky, David thought.

"I think it was lucky you came to spend the summer with us," Gert told her. "I enjoy your company very much."

"My friend Betty from violin class calls you a shrink. Is that a bad word?"

"No, that's just a word people use for *psychiatrist.* So you see, when I said I was just going to shrink away, I didn't know then that I'd actually wind up still working as a shrink. I'm glad you've found a friend."

Sarah, who was too young to grasp the nuances of shrinking away, continued to chatter on about Betty. Under the cover of her voice, David said to Amy, "You're quiet."

"I was eavesdropping on the two in back."

"Can we turn on some music, Daddy?" Sarah asked. "Ms. Archer said we should listen to music and try to hear the violins."

"Sure. We'll all listen for them," David said.

At the reservation, he parked at the Bearclaw ranch. As they got out, Sage came running toward them, still lanky at twelve, but showing traces of the woman she'd one day become. "Hey," she said to them. After David introduced Sage and Amy, Sage focused on Sarah.

Holding out her hand, she said, "We found some powwow clothes to fit you. Come with me and you can try them on."

After seeing her father nod, Sarah didn't hesitate to go ahead with Sage.

Amy looked at David, sharing his pleased smile at Sarah's improved self-confidence. "Are powwow clothes special?" she asked as they walked toward the house.

"Western is fine, so your denim skirt fits right in," David said.

Shane Bearclaw and his wife, Laura, greeted them cordially. Amy responded, but her attention was fixed on the impressive old man whose braids hung down onto an elaborate beaded buckskin shirt. Grandfather?

After he handed the little boy he held to Shane, his dark gaze caught hers and he examined her with obvious interest, finally smiling at her. "You're Amy," he said. "Even in my hawk dream you had green eyes."

Unsure how to respond, she finally said, "I've heard about that dream."

"When you're ready, I'll tell it to you. Today, we'll share the powwow." He held out a feathered band. "For your wrist."

As she was fastening hers in place, she saw him hand another, slightly different, to David, who put it around his wrist. Sage appeared with Sarah, both decked out in colorful costumes.

Grandfather then announced, "It's time to go."

They followed Shane's truck past a beautiful lake set among a strange-to-Amy landscape with no trees, only rocks and sparse desert growth. Odd-shaped formations rose above the water here and there.

"I almost feel like I'm on the moon," she said.

"My teacher told us there's no water on the moon," Sarah informed her, making them all smile.

Parked cars and trucks crowded together near a large frame building. Color and sounds assailed Amy's eyes and ears as they approached it on foot. The delicious smell of what David told her was Indian fry bread cooking made her mouth water. Sage and Grandfather found them, taking both Sarah and Gert away "for the dancing."

Amy was amazed. "Does he mean Gert actually participates in the Paiute dances?"

David nodded. "She says it's a way of renewing one's life force."

"So people who aren't Native Americans can dance with the Paiutes?"

"If they're sponsored by one and if they try to learn not only the steps, but the meaning of the dances."

Aware the dances had a spiritual basis, Amy wondered if Sarah was old enough to understand this. Or if she'd be too afraid to try to dance because of her leg. She loved the sandals and sneakers with the lifts

David had arranged for, but dancing in them was another matter altogether. Sarah obviously had been overcome with instant admiration for Sage, but would it be enough to overcome her fear of being ridiculed?

"Laura Bearclaw seems young to have a daughter as old as Sage," Amy said.

"Sage is Shane's half sister. Different fathers. The boy is Shane and Laura's, though."

The Bearclaws had all looked relaxed and happy. Amy tried to suppress the twinge she often felt when confronted with what appeared to be a well-adjusted family. She realized appearances weren't necessarily the truth, but somehow she'd sensed a true connection between the Bearclaws. Her own family hadn't been dysfunctional exactly, but... She sighed.

Looking up, she found David eyeing her quizzically. "Something wrong?"

"Not really."

He seemed about to question that when an earsplitting whistle startled them both. An insistent drumming began. People began to drift toward the building, so they followed suit. When they'd nearly reached the open doors, a woman called David's name and he paused. Amy watched as one of the most gorgeous women she'd ever seen threw her arms around him and gave him a hug.

"So good to see you," she told him when she stepped back.

"It's been a long time." He turned to Amy. "This is Jessica Patsona. Amy Simon."

Jessica, tall, dark and sleek, smiled at Amy. "I

heard Gert had taken on an associate.'' Glancing at David, she said, ''How lucky for you.''

David grinned at her. ''Where are you working these days?''

Jessica grimaced. ''Chicago. The Midwest isn't my favorite place. Or maybe what I mean is the people I'm dealing with right now don't rate high in my book. You're looking good.''

He shrugged.

Switching her attention to Amy, Jessica evaluated her with her gaze. ''Must be you're the key that switched him from off to on. And high time, too. I'm glad we met. See you later.'' With that, Jessica tunneled into the crowd and vanished.

''She's got a point,'' David said. ''I'm definitely turned on.''

By her or by me? Amy wondered sourly, then shook her head as though to erase the thought. True, Jessica was at least a ten, but it wasn't even remotely possible that Amy Simon could be jealous. Never. To be jealous implied heavy-duty emotions, a deep involvement with David. Chemistry, yes, anything else, no.

So why did she find herself asking, ''How long have you known Jessica?''

''We met at last year's powwow. She's not home much—works as an associate for a Frisco firm that sends her around the country.''

''Wow, I would have said a model.''

''Yeah, she's got the looks. A classy gal.''

The next question was how well had he known her, but that was one she'd bite her tongue off before asking, considering the words were as green with jealousy as Jessica's striking eyes.

As though aware of her thoughts, he said, "I didn't remember her eyes were green, too. Different shade than yours, though."

"Daddy, Daddy." Sarah's excited voice cut through Amy's unwelcome musing. "Come watch. Sage taught me the kid's dance and I can do it." She grasped David's hand and urged him forward.

David caught Amy's hand and pulled her along with him.

Inside, a large central area had been roped off and colorfully costumed children were gathering there. Sarah, who was wearing her own denim skirt with faux silver ornaments, had exchanged her white T-shirt for a beaded one with a hand-painted rabbit in the center. Her brown hair was held back with a thong that had silver and red ribbons threaded through it.

"You look like you really belong among the dancers," Amy told her as they made their way to the center ring.

"Sage said I'm supposed to think about being part of everything around me when I dance," Sarah confided. "Like that lake and the rocks and the sky and the animals."

"Good idea," David told her.

"I'm going to think about Sheba, too," Sarah said as she ducked under the rope and hurried to where Sage was standing.

"How is the kitten?" Amy asked David.

"Eyes open, tumbling around with her siblings. Smaller than them, but just as feisty."

Amy stood watching with David as the children began their dance. Boys first, then girls. She spotted Sarah, wearing a fierce frown of concentration, but noticed her expression brightening as the girls continued to circle the ring, dancing in time to the rhythm of the drums.

"She's starting to enjoy herself," Amy murmured, as proud of the girl as if she'd been her own.

David squeezed her hand, making her aware they were still holding hands like any couple in love.

Whoa. Back up, girl. Love has no place in this twosome. But she left her hand in his.

When the children finished, the men danced, then the women, Gert among them, looking supremely self-confident, as usual. Jessica, her exotic beauty heightened by her Paiute costume, was right behind Gert.

"They all dance separately," Amy commented.

"Jessica told me that's because dance steps differ for men and women. So does the reason for the dances."

Jessica again. Well, so what?

"After this is over we'll grab something to eat before the couples dancing starts," he added. "I recommend the buffalo tacos."

Outside, they connected with Sage and Sarah long enough to buy food for the kids, then Sage led Sarah off again, promising to meet them in an hour and a half. After she and David finished eating, Amy bought hand-made obsidian wind chimes from one of the Paiute vendors and they detoured to leave the chimes in Gert's car. By the time they returned to the building, music drifted on a wind tinged with the faint smell of sage.

Though they'd never danced together before, Amy already knew how well she fitted in David's arms. Public place or not, at his touch the same tingle of desire trickled through her. "Been waiting for this," he whispered in her ear.

She floated dreamily through two numbers before Grandfather insisted it was his turn to dance with her. David whirled off with his aunt, leaving her with the old medicine man, who turned out to be a talented dancer.

"In my dream, the hawk with green eyes didn't know her own heart," he told her. "She was a stubborn bird, determined to fly off in a certain direction, as if her choice was the only path. We all are faced with many paths and the truest way to choose is with the heart."

Taken aback, she stammered, "I don't—I'm not sure I understand."

"My heart tells me you are the hawk from my dream."

Amy gathered her wits. "Because of my green eyes? Aren't Jessica Patsona's also green?"

Grandfather sighed. "Like you, Jessica has yet to understand her heart, but she was not my dream hawk."

He spoke softly, yet the finality in his tone convinced her he believed what he said whether she did or not. Like all prophecies, it was vague enough so that she could interpret his words however she chose.

She was about to say so when Grandfather said,

"The male hawk was David, also flying in his own stubborn direction. I will warn him, too." He sighed again. "Why is it the young have no ears to hear?"

Shortly after this, Shane Bearclaw claimed a dance with her, leaving Grandfather with Laura.

Shane was as gorgeous a man as Jessica was a woman. It occurred to Amy that he and she might have grown up together, so she asked him.

"Jessica was younger," he said. "I knew her, but we didn't run with the same crowd as kids." He grinned down at Amy. "Mine was wilder." His smile faded. "I came back to the res when I got it through my thick head I belonged here. She stays away."

"Isn't that all right?"

He shrugged, frustrating her. Why did men so often insist on letting questions roll off their shoulders? David was a prime offender.

As if she'd said the name out loud, Shane said, "David's looking good."

Jessica's words. Before she realized what she meant to do, she snapped, "It's my opinion as a psychologist that he's still in denial."

Shane held her away from him a little, staring down at her with elevated eyebrows. "Denial of what?"

Already regretting her words, she muttered, "Well, law, for one thing. He won't face the fact that's what he really wants to do."

"You're treating him?" Shane's voice held a certain chill.

"No," she said hurriedly. "If I was, I would never have talked about his problem."

"So your opinion is that of a friend who happens to be a psychologist."

She nodded, sorry she'd brought up the subject.

"David's my friend, too," Shane said. "I work with mustangs—Nevada's wild horses—and they've taught me patience, among other things. If it's in David's heart to return to law, he will. If not, he won't. Pushing him won't work."

"You sound like Grandfather."

"I should, he trained me." With that, Shane swung her around, intercepting David, who was dancing with Jessica. "Time for a change," he said.

Moments later Amy was back in David's arms, but now it wasn't the same. "I need a breather," she said.

He led her off the floor and out of the building.

"You don't need to come with me," she told him.

"What if I want to?"

Before she could answer, Sage and Sarah ran up. "Can I stay at Sage's house tonight?" Sarah asked. "Her brother has to drive into Gardnerville tomorrow to drop off some of the stuff he makes for a gift shop, so he'll take me to Tourmaline first."

David glanced at Amy, but she didn't indicate her opinion in any way. This was his decision to make.

"Do you really want to, punkin?" he asked.

"That's *citrouille*, Daddy," she said, giggling as she looked at Amy.

Not wanting to disappoint the girl, Amy forced a smile. "That's exactly what it is, Sarah."

"What's with you two?" he demanded.

"French," Sarah said between giggles.

"French," he echoed. Then he grinned. "For *pumpkin,* you mean. Just you wait till I get even."

"I want to stay with Sage," Sarah said excitedly. "She's got her very own horse that she raised from a baby and I haven't even seen him yet."

"It's okay with my brother and Laura," Sage said. "Dr. Gert's going to stay over, too, so she'll be riding in with Sarah and Shane tomorrow."

Leaving David and me alone together, Amy thought. A coincidence that seems to be happening a lot lately—or am I getting paranoid? Surely Gert wouldn't be so obvious.

"Have fun," David told Sarah.

"I will. Bye, Daddy."

"Don't I get a hug?"

Sarah hugged him, then held out her arms to Amy, who knelt and hugged her.

As they watched the two girls run off together, Amy found herself worrying that Sarah might wake in the night and be homesick for her father and familiar surroundings. She shut off the thought. If it happened, Gert was there to reassure the girl. In any case, Sarah wasn't her responsibility, even if her heart didn't agree. Which reminded her of Grandfather's hawks.

"Grandfather said you were the male hawk in his dream," she told David.

"I know. Gert told me."

"Well, it turns out I'm the female hawk and both of us are flying off in the wrong direction."

"Together?"

"I don't think so."

"Too bad. No point in worrying about it, since we're together at the moment."

Did she want to be alone with David right now? Before she came up with an answer, he grasped her hand, leading her toward Gert's car. "We'll drive down to the lake," he said.

She started to bristle at his assumption that's what she wanted to do, but let it go since that seemed as good a place as any for the discussion they needed to have.

It was near dusk when he parked by Pyramid Lake. The space between dusk and night was shorter here in Nevada than it had been in California because the Sierras were to the west, so the sun disappeared behind them before dropping into the Pacific. She avoided holding his hand as they walked down to the water in the alpenglow, an orange-pink radiance that lit the western sky above the mountains and briefly held back the dark.

"This lake is so different from Tahoe," she said.

"Small talk," he muttered, brushing it away with a sweep of his hand.

She looked at him and found him scowling at her.

"What the hell is the matter with you?" he demanded.

She knew as a psychologist that "nothing," was not the right answer. As a woman, though, she was tempted. Taking a deep breath, she tried to order her thoughts, but they remained in such chaos that she found herself asking the one thing she hadn't meant to say but really wanted to know. "Did you and Jessica have an affair?"

He stared at her.

Amy met his gaze as calmly as she could, holding back her apology, even though she knew she had no right to ask that question since it was none of her business. She shouldn't have said it, but she already had. Let him try to shrug that one off.

His "No" was clipped.

"Oh" was the only thing she could think of to say in reply.

"Have I ever asked you about any of your affairs?" His tone was brusque.

"I only had one that could qualify for the term," she snapped. "It convinced me never to trust a man again."

"You're saying you don't trust me?"

"Yes. No. I mean, I don't know. It doesn't matter, anyway, since we're not lovers."

"We will be." He spit the words out between clenched teeth.

"You don't sound happy about it."

"I'm not."

She scowled at him. "Neither am I."

All of a sudden the ridiculous nature of their exchange struck her and she began to laugh. After a long moment, he joined in. As they laughed together, she was dimly aware a truck had stopped somewhere near them. When she could speak again, ignoring the truck, she said, "I recall words from an old song that say something like, never lovers, always friends. That might be best."

"You have the words wrong—it's always lovers, never friends."

"I don't think so."

"Neither is quite right." Gert's voice came out of the gathering darkness.

They both turned to look at her. "What are the words, then?" David asked.

"You don't need them to work things out. I came to tell you that Sarah and I are leaving now with the Bearclaws. Good night." With that she turned and started back up the rise.

"You shrinks leave more questions unanswered," he commented.

"Forces you to reflect," Gert called back. "Good for the spirit."

"It's time we were getting back, too," Amy said to him.

Once they were on their way to Tourmaline, David said, "Any ideas about next Saturday?"

He was consulting her, a definite improvement. "I called my brother earlier this week and we have an open invitation to their place. Since Sarah seemed so interested in Sage's horse, I think she'll be enthusiastic about riding a pony."

"Great. So that's on for a week from now. But there's still tonight. Without Sarah."

"I'm aware of that."

His next words showed he'd detected the dismissal in her voice. "Too calculated?"

"Not exactly, but…" Her words trailed off as she realized she didn't really know why she disliked the notion of planning ahead for a night of passion. Did it somehow date back to college and that miserable time with Vince when any lovemaking had to be scheduled because he was so busy? Her lip twisted in remembered humiliation. *Penciled in* was the right term, so it could be erased if necessary. What a fool she'd been.

"I can easily arrange to throw you over my shoulder, haul you to my cave and have my way with you."

Despite herself, his teasing words sent a thrill through her. Never mind her dislike of control, somewhere buried inside her that sort of fantasy must exist. Not that she actually wanted it to happen.

"It's not that simple," she told him.

"No? Seems pretty straightforward to me."

"It does have the advantage of surprise," she admitted, "but it doesn't allow the woman any say."

"You just said no to any other arrangement." As he spoke, he pulled the car onto the shoulder, shut off the engine, released both seat-belts and yanked her willy-nilly into his arms. When his mouth slanted down over hers, she discovered that she'd seriously underestimated just how much she wanted him.

Not that her passion meter was an accurate measure of what was best for her. With a tremendous effort of will, she broke away.

Without a word, David restarted the car, pulled back on the highway and drove, way too fast, toward Tourmaline.

Chapter Nine

On Wednesday evening David opened his apartment door to see Amy standing there. "I come bearing gifts," she said. "My famous, if we're lucky, chocolate chip oatmeal cookies—on other occasions known as infamous."

"Amy!" Sarah cried. "Come and see how big Sheba's getting."

"By all means," David said, ushering her in. He'd missed her, but he damn well didn't mean to say so. Not after last Saturday night, when they'd parted without even a good-night kiss.

Amy wound up holding the kitten while Sarah played her latest violin lesson. David noticed her wince only once, a confirmation of his opinion that Sarah was improving.

"That was so good you deserve cookies and milk," Amy said when she finished.

As they sat in the kitchen, Amy and David with coffee, Sarah said, "Daddy says I'm going to get to ride a pony Saturday. All by myself. I never have before."

"It's lots easier than riding a camel," Amy assured her.

"I'm not too worried." David and Amy exchanged smiles at her assumption of nonchalance.

It felt right to have Amy around, the attention she gave to Sarah made the three of them a family in a way he'd never felt with Iris. Uneasy with the thought, he shoved it away.

"Sometime can Betty go with us?" Sarah asked. "Her father doesn't get home very much."

"Not this Saturday, but another time, if it's okay with her mother," David said.

The phone rang. David picked it up. "Speaking," he said.

"They what?" he asked, listened, then added, "Call the sheriff. I'll be right over."

"That was the woman who saw Cal's accident," he told Amy. "Will you stay with Sarah?"

"Sure, but how about dropping off Sarah with Gert so I can tag along? I could hear that woman—not words, but she sounded hysterical. I might be able to help."

David hesitated, then nodded. Dodie Thomas would need to calm down before he had any chance of talking sense with her.

Once they'd left Sarah at Gert's, Amy asked what had happened.

"I talked to Dodie Thomas soon after Cal gave me her name. She was clearly too frightened to tell me much of anything, but I told her to call me if she changed her mind. Right after I was there, she began to get threatening phone calls and finally let me know about them. I insisted she call the sheriff's department, sort of bullied her into it. They advised her to get caller ID and change her number, which took care of the problem. Last week I went over to her place at her request, and while I was there, someone threw a rock through her front window. I called the sheriff, telling the deputy I was her lawyer, and that I suspected someone was trying to intimidate my client."

"Could they do anything?"

David shook his head. "Now, this evening, a neighbor saw a van run up onto her side lawn, aiming at her dog, which was tied to a post."

"Oh, no! I hope they didn't hit the poor thing."

"He was injured—the neighbor's taking him to a vet."

"How awful. All this just so she wouldn't testify against them about the accident?"

"Looks that way. I found out the driver who hit Cal has a criminal record."

Amy felt hurt that David hadn't told her any of this earlier, but realized she'd probably brought it on herself by too many "shrink" questions.

A sheriff's deputy was at the Thomas house when they arrived, trying to get a coherent story from Dodie, who, face streaked with tears, was running her fingers frantically through her hair. He greeted them with relief. Amy persuaded Dodie into the bathroom where she helped her wash her face and brush her hair.

"I'm being punished," Dodie told her. "Ma always said, 'Tell the truth and shame the devil,' but I took the truth back 'cause I let those men scare me. Now my little Susu's going to die."

"Susu's at the vet's getting the best of care," Amy said soothingly. She handed Dodie a glass of water, adding, "Crying always makes me thirsty."

"Yeah, I guess it does at that."

Some minutes later, a much calmer Dodie was back in the living room able to corroborate the story David had told the deputy. "I'm going to tell the truth this time," she assured the deputy. "I couldn't believe it last month when I saw that van veer over deliberately to hit that poor man on the motorcycle. But that's what they did. On purpose, too. Just like they tried to kill my Susu."

She looked at David. "I'll help your friend Cal by telling what I saw. You let him know, will you?"

"I'll take care of it. Thanks."

"Would you like to come and spend the night with me?" Amy asked her.

Dodie shook her head. "That's real nice of you, but I'm sort of over being scared. Pete, next door, already said he'd lend me his rottweiler. Nobody messes with that mutt."

"Your neighbor gave me the license number of the van that hit your dog," the deputy said. "I doubt you'll have any more trouble tonight."

While she and David were driving to Gert's to pick up Sarah, Amy asked, ''Do you think the case will come to court?''

''A trial, you mean? I doubt it.''

''You helped your friend, and Dodie Thomas, too.'' She wanted to add how wonderful she thought he was for going out of his way to do so, but she worried that he might think she was trying to sneak in some therapy, so all she said was, ''You're a good guy.''

The next morning, as she was leaving for work, she found a note on her door. ''Susu survived with a broken leg.'' She smiled, tucking the paper into her bag. David hadn't signed it, but she intended to keep her one and only note from him.

She felt good about what she saw as his beginning reconciliation with the legal profession. He'd gone to bat for Cal, hadn't he? She was sure that, if necessary, he'd represent Cal in court. He might still be in denial, but each time he helped someone sort out a legal mess, she believed he drew closer to returning to the profession he'd once loved.

Amy sang along with the radio all the way to Gert's. Just wait until she sprang her wonderful surprise on him this weekend.

On Saturday, Russ and Mari Simon greeted Amy, David and Sarah with enthusiasm. ''Elias is out by the corral,'' Russ said. ''He can't wait to show off his pony to Sarah.''

''So let's join him there, then,'' Amy said after setting down a small bag on the porch.

As they made their way to the corral, David looked around at Amy's brother's layout, startled when he saw the size of the horses in a nearby field. "Those are big ones. Amy didn't mention you bred draft horses."

"They may look gray, but they're actually Blues," Mari told them. "Elias's pony, Buddy, is a dapple-gray, though."

"That's the pony's name, Buddy?" Sarah asked.

Mari smiled at her. "Yes, and he's as friendly as his name sounds. Actually we have a second pony now, a chestnut mare named Cheri."

"Is that a French word?" Sarah asked.

"How smart of you," Mari said. "Yes, it means dear."

"Amy's got a French dictionary. She taught me the word for pumpkin and how to say hello and good-bye."

Three-year-old Elias was sitting on the fence under the watchful eye of a ranch hand propped against the fence beside him. He lifted the boy down and Elias ran to meet them.

"You're Sarah," he said, coming to a stop in front of her.

"And you're Elias," she said. "Hi."

"You can ride one of my ponies," he told her.

"Buddy or Cheri?"

"Cheri 'cause she's a girl. She's my sister's pony, 'cept Izzy's too little to ride."

"That's short for Isabel, in case you wondered," Mari said. "She's three months old."

David led Sarah to where the ranch hand held the

lead of the chestnut pony, lifted her into the saddle and stood there with his hand bracing her. "Okay?" he asked.

"She's not nearly so high up as the camel," Sarah said, sounding relieved.

Russ settled Elias on the gray pony, then moved to shorten the stirrups on the chestnut to fit Sarah. "You take hold of the reins," he told her. "Hank, here, is going to lead the pony and he'll tell you what to do with the reins. This is your first time so Cheri will stay on the lead. When you've ridden a couple times you'll be ready to try it on your own."

"You mean I get to come back here?" she asked.

"Anytime you want," Russ assured her.

She beamed at him, making David smile at her obvious pleasure.

They all settled either on the fence or leaning against it to watch the children walk the ponies around the riding ring, Elias on his own.

David heard Mari say to Amy, "The keys are up at the house. Whenever you want to go, just say the word."

Glancing at Amy, he asked, "Go where?"

"It's a secret." She slid off the fence and walked over to where Sarah was riding, matching her pace to the pony's while she asked the girl something in such a low tone that he couldn't quite catch the words.

"It's okay with me," Sarah replied. "I like it here." She looked at her father and waved. "Bye, Daddy," she said. "Have fun."

Have fun. Words he'd often said to Sarah these past

weeks. And today she was clearly enjoying herself. He waved back at his daughter.

Amy took his hand, and as she led him away from the corral toward the house, they were joined by Mari. "Too bad Isabel's napping, you'll have to wait till next time to say hello to her. Don't worry about Sarah. She'll be fine with us. Elias was thrilled to know she was coming. We'll expect you when we see you."

When they were back in his pickup, David said, "I suppose you're going to drag out this surprise stuff."

"What else? Go back to the highway and turn toward Genoa. Russ says we can pick up Kingsbury Grade there, if you know what that is."

"We're going to Lake Tahoe?"

She grinned at him. "Jackpot."

"Which brings sailing to mind. But I don't have a boat."

"My lips are sealed."

He slanted her a mock frown. "What if I don't like surprises?"

"Then you'll be out of luck, won't you? How did you like my brother's ranch?"

"Nice spread."

"I adore Mari—he was so fortunate to find her. His first wife was the pits."

"She run off with someone?"

"Not with anyone, but she did run off when he decided he wanted to raise horses."

"I remember you saying he chose horses over law. Lucky guy."

"Don't tell me you're going to start a horse ranch?" She actually sounded alarmed.

Unable to resist, he looked at her straightfaced and said, "No, I was thinking of pigs."

She turned to stare at him. "You *what?*"

He couldn't keep the grin back and she scowled at him. "I'll get you for that."

"You take things too seriously. Stop being an analyst on your time off. Gert manages to."

"True." She sighed. After a moment, she added, "Tell you what—the rest of this day I'll do my best to be frivolous."

"I like the sound of that. I'd like it still more if Frivolous Amy would tell me what she's going to be frivolous doing."

"You are one impatient man. A few more miles and we'll be in Incline Village. Then all will be revealed."

"Our destination is Incline, then, not this side of the lake."

She nodded.

As they approached the village she directed his turns until he found himself in the parking area of what looked to be a new and upscale condominium complex.

"Do you have instructions on where to park, too?" he asked, noting that all the slots were marked.

"Mari says her grandfather owns garage number one, so we can park in there."

"We're going to visit Mari's grandfather?"

"Not quite."

David shrugged and pulled in front of the garage

marked with a number one. "The door's closed. Now what?"

Amy pointed a key at the garage and pushed a button on it. Inside was a white Jag, with room for David's truck next to it. Amy took care of closing the door and they exited through a breezeway to the complex proper, which required the use of another key to enter. Faced with two closed elevator doors, David said, "I assume we go up."

She shot him a triumphant grin. "No, actually we go down to get to the surprise. Use the elevator to the left."

"If you say so."

Inside, she pushed a button and the elevator dropped down. The doors opened, and through the windows of the lounge they came out into, David could see a small marina.

Amy hurried past him to throw open a door to the outside. "Voilà!" she cried.

David followed her out. Standing on a wooden dock, he stared up at the most graceful sailboat he'd ever seen, the *Frivolous*. He burst out laughing. "We're even," he told Amy.

"Mari's grandfather said we could use the boat whenever we liked. He's at his cottage on Mackinac Island right now, so this is a good time."

David's gaze drifted from the boat back to the rise of the condominium. He thought about the penthouse elevator and the cottage on Mackinac Island. "Just who is her grandfather?"

"Oh, I guess I assumed you knew he was Joseph Haskell."

David shook his head. Everyone knew who Joe Haskell was, and he vaguely recalled something a couple of years ago about the man finding a long-lost granddaughter. "Your brother is married to the Haskell heir?" he asked.

She nodded. "Mari doesn't think of herself like that. You must have been able to see she doesn't."

Amy was right, he'd liked Mari from the start. "So we're going to sail the *Frivolous* into the blue waters of Lake Tahoe. You've surprised me, all right." He looked up at the boat again. "It'll take both of us to handle her."

Grinning at him, she said, "That's why I brought you along—I knew I couldn't do it alone."

"Sure. And I'm the gingerbread man."

Amy's eyebrows rose. "The gingerbread man?"

David knew where he'd gotten the words, knew, too, why they'd popped into his mind. A year ago he'd actually thought of himself as the gingerbread man, running, running as fast as he can. In place.

"It's a story Sarah liked read to her when she was little." He recalled now that he'd had the time to read to his daughter when she was a toddler, before he joined Murdock's firm, a move Iris had urged him to make. A mistake. Still, couldn't he have made time for Sarah?

"Time to go aboard," he told Amy, wiping the past from his mind.

"Aye, aye, captain."

After Amy helped him hoist the sails, he used the motor to ease the *Frivolous* from her slip and out of the condo marina into the lake, where he shut it off.

Wind filled the sails, sending them gliding almost
soundlessly except for occasional creaks, flaps and the
splash of waves against the hull. Sunlight glittered on
the blue water and a lone seagull circled above as
they left Incline Village behind for the sail across to
Emerald Bay.

The day was perfect for sailing, enough wind to
send the boat scudding along, but not strong enough
so it became a threat. As usual, the big mountain lake
wasn't crowded with boats. By the time they were
well out, the *Frivolous* might as well have been alone
on the water, since no other boats were in sight.

"What a glorious day," Amy said. After a moment, she added, "The water is so blue here, why do
they call it Emerald Bay?"

Looking at her, he was tempted to say, "Because
it matches your beautiful green eyes." He told himself he didn't because, at the moment, she wore sun-
glasses, as he did. But he knew the reason was that
he didn't want to sound ridiculously romantic, even
though he felt that way at the moment. Which had to
do with the day and the boat as much as it did the
woman. At least that's what he'd like to believe.

"You'll see when we get there," he told her.

"No old tale to go with the reason?"

"There's an island in the bay where someone built
a tea house, so her guests who were staying in the
mansion on the shore, could sail over, climb the hill
and have tea served in the little house."

Amy rolled her eyes. "Not my kind of tale. No
romantic meetings of doomed lovers, no unsolved
crimes. No hauntings. Is the tea house still there?"

"Remnants."

"Oh well, then. Ruins are romantic."

"I didn't take you for a hopeless romantic."

"That's the way I felt about my brother before he met Mari. But you're correct, I'm really not."

Which was the truth, Amy told herself. She'd had every vestige of romance permanently eradicated after her experience with Vince. Betrayal will crush a lot of feelings.

"That's right, you don't trust men."

"Those I've met haven't given me any reason to." She heard the sadness in her voice with dismay.

"One in particular." It wasn't a question.

How could he be so sure? She was certain she wasn't that easy to read. "It's water under the bridge, down the river, over the dam and into the sea."

The wind, picking up, caught the sails, sending the boat flying. It laid over, skimming the waves, sending a thrill of pure elation tingling through her. She'd forgotten the joy of sailing. Forgotten a lot of things, like the wonder of a perfect day spent with the right man. Tomorrow aside, at this moment David *was* the right man to be with.

They reached Emerald Bay as the sun was lowering. As she marveled at how the water changed color to a brilliant green, he said, "One problem. The wind won't favor us on the way back. Plus, the way it's beginning to blow, we'd be at risk." He gave her a rueful grin. "Something like running out of gas for the truck at the dead end of a lonesome mountain road. Only in this case, too much wind, not none, is the problem."

"You mean we can't get back?"

"Not before dark, which means we'd have night as well as the rising wind to contend with. I'm going to look for a cove to anchor in."

"As Sarah's friend Betty would say—awesome. Marooned for the night on Emerald Bay."

"You sound as if you don't mind."

She shrugged. "Neither of us have to go to work tomorrow and Sarah's perfectly safe at my brother's." No way did she intend to admit right now that she'd brought the pj's and the change of clothes always left at Gert's for Sarah, along with them to her brother's—just in case. "Besides, I've never spent a night on a boat before."

"You've never spent a night with me, either," he said.

They exchanged a long look before having to busy themselves with lowering the sails and the other tasks necessary to anchoring. While she worked, excitement mixed with a thread of anxiety hummed through Amy.

From the beginning, planning this outing, she'd realized this might be the outcome. She'd thought of it as an end to her indecision, her wishy-washy behavior toward a relationship with David, but now that the time was here, she teetered on the verge of wondering if she'd made the right choice. For it would be a commitment of sorts, she saw that plainly.

"What's the matter?" David asked. "All of a sudden you look scared. The boat's in no danger anchored here for the night. We're safe enough."

He saw too much and yet not quite enough. She

took a deep breath, mustered up a saucy look and said, "Are we?"

David smiled. "Looking at it that way, maybe not. But I'd say we've finally reached the right place at the right time to find out."

That was what she needed—to find out. Not about their coming together, she knew in her very bones that part of it would be a success. But could she handle an intense relationship that would probably go nowhere? Up until now she'd been too much of a coward to attempt it. That was before she'd met David, though, and the fire between them couldn't be ignored. He'd brought her the need to know.

Why didn't he wrap his arms around her right this minute and banish all her doubts?

Instead, he went calmly on with putting the boat to rights, just as though he'd spent night after night anchored on Emerald Bay with her and so already knew everything there was to know about what would happen.

He leaned toward her and her breath caught. Had he sensed her thoughts?

"Have you checked the galley?" he asked. "What are we having for dinner?"

She couldn't help glaring at him.

He straightened. "Hey, I intend to help, not sit around and be waited on."

"That's not the point." She stalked over to the cabin entrance and eased herself down into it. She was about to open a cupboard and peer inside, when he grabbed her from behind and rolled her onto one of the bunks.

"Been waiting all day for this," he said, holding her close, his lips a breath away from hers. "Couldn't figure out a way to get you down here any sooner, though."

Chapter Ten

Sprawled on the bunk in the boat cabin, for a moment Amy lost herself in David's embrace, then she squirmed free. "Food first," she declared.

"Food last," he growled, reaching for her again.

She stood, moving out of reach. "Haven't you heard anticipation gives everything an extra edge?" she teased. Now that she knew he was as strung up as she was, she decided it might be fun to prolong things.

"Edge? Woman, what do you think I'm teetering on?"

She opened the door of the small refrigerator, saying, "You said you'd help with—oh, wow!"

He got to his feet and peered over her shoulder.

"Mari said her grandfather's housekeeper would see to it the boat was stocked and ready," Amy said, "but this is an entire gourmet feast." She reached in, took a shrimp, dipped it in sauce and turned. "Open your mouth."

When he did, she popped in the shrimp.

"I could go for a couple more," he admitted after he finished it. Then he sat down, took off his sneakers and socks and wriggled his toes. "Ah, freedom at last."

He looked so comfortable, she decided to do the same before setting the table.

With the sun beginning to sink behind the Sierras, the cabin grew dark so David lit the lamps. He turned on a CD player as Amy set the food she found in the refrigerator on the table. Also inside chilling were two stemmed glasses and a bottle from a select New York winery.

"What shall we drink to?" she asked when they were both seated at the table listening to what had to be big band music from Joe Haskell's time—the thirties and forties.

"To Gert," David said, raising his glass, "with thanks."

As she sipped her wine, Amy tried to tell herself she wasn't disappointed. Then again, had she really expected the toast to be "to us" or something similar? By the time she'd eaten her way through the shrimp and started on the cold salmon mousse, though, she realized it may have been his roundabout way of saying, "to us." After all, if it hadn't been for Gert, they never would have met. As to the future, David could be no more sure than she was what "us" would prove to mean to either of them.

After they were through eating, David helped her tidy the cabin and then they went up on deck. The wind had died down, the full moon, big and beautiful, sent silver dancing across the water and pine-scented evening air slid across the skin like silk. Below, a singer crooned about dancing in the dark.

"Shall we?" David asked her, holding out his arms.

She moved into them and they glided across the deck. Amy tingled from his touch, warmth pooling inside her from the feel of his body pressed against hers. Before this moment she had never thought dancing with a man could be so arousing. Was it because they were alone and anything might happen?

The vocalist sang something about forever and she nestled closer, wishing this moment could last until the end of time. Eventually she grew aware another song was playing, a singer asking whether it could be nothing but moon love. *Moon love.* The words echoed in her mind. Love was too scary a feeling to contemplate, but moon love, something born of the magic of the night, something that might not last, but would be wonderful while it did, was somehow a lighter emotion, one she could catch hold of.

"If we carry on with anticipating much longer," David whispered in her ear, "I'm warning you, the deck's damn hard." As he spoke, he eased toward the opening of the cabin, leaving it up to her to choose.

A shaft of moonlight seemed to beckon her down the steps. In the cabin, one lamp still burned. She turned and looked at David, seeing her own hunger reflected in his eyes.

"I've been counting the seven buttons on your shirt all day," he said, "wondering how long it takes to undo them."

"You've only got two buttons on your polo shirt and they're already undone," she countered.

"You could pull it over my head."

She did just that, and though she'd seen his naked chest more than once, her heart accelerated.

He reached and undid the top button of her shirt, murmuring, "Seven." One by one he unbuttoned, counting down until he reached the last. "Off," he concluded, and eased the shirt from her shoulders. She gasped as he molded his hands over the pale green silk of her bra cups, her nipples rising, aching for his touch.

He reached around her, unfastened the hook, slid off the straps and tossed her bra aside. She heard his breath catch as he gazed at her breasts. "Your turn," he rasped.

She had trouble unhooking the silver buckle of his belt, but it finally came free. Her fingers fumbled at the top snap, got it open and slowly slid down the zipper, the hardness she could feel as she did so sending pulsating waves from her fingertips to her groin. He slid down the jeans, flung them away and reached to undo hers. He hadn't even kissed her yet, but the act of undressing each other appealed so erotically to her that she could feel herself melting inside.

She stepped out of her jeans, cast them aside and hooked her fingers under the waistband of his shorts. Once she'd eased them down, she stared at the marked evidence of how ready he was, sparks of anticipation crackling through her.

He disposed of her bikinis in a single swoop, lifted her into his arms, laid her gently onto the double bunk and eased down beside her, gathering her to him and kissing her at last.

The kiss, deep and hard and demanding, drew a wild and abandoned response from her. She could sense herself on the edge of losing control, of giving herself up to pure feeling, letting it take her where it would. Since, even in the better days with Vince, she'd always remained in control of herself, a sliver of fear tensed her for an instant.

But David's warm caresses soon disposed of the sliver, stealing away the remnants of her control, sending her circling upward on a thermal of passion, higher and higher.

"Now, oh, please now," she heard someone pleading breathlessly, unsure if it was her.

He took her higher still before he joined with her, skyrocketing her into their own private realm of pleasure. When they'd glided down into reality again, he shifted to his side, still holding her in his arms. "You were right," he murmured.

"About what?"

"That was some extra edge."

Extra edge or not, not too many minutes passed before he bent his head to her breast, starting a new burst of sensation along her nerve endings. This time she had the chance to savor the sensuous feel of his bare skin against hers as they made slow, sweet love, ending in an equally mind-shattering climax.

Afterward they lay side by side, her hand in his, a sheet pulled over them. She was drifting between awake and asleep, when he said, "You said you look like your chorus girl great-grandmother. If she was anything like you otherwise, no wonder your great-grandfather defied the family for her."

"I guess that's a compliment."

"You know it." He leaned over and kissed her, then settled back down. "That was the first part of kiss and tell. Your turn."

"What do you mean my turn?"

"Some bastard made you mistrust men."

Bastard described Vince perfectly. But he was better left in the past. "What if I don't want to tell?"

"Isn't the right word *denial?*"

"Just who's the shrink here, anyway?"

He chuckled. "Don't like the tables turned, do you?"

"Okay, so he was a guy I met my first year in college. I was taking pre-law then, but he was already in law school. I was naive. He wasn't. It was a painful lesson. End of story."

"Is he the one who drove you out of pre-law into psych?"

Amy thought about it. "Not exactly. He hastened the switch, since after Vince I realized I didn't want to be a lawyer. I never had, actually. But my dad brainwashed me just like he did Russ. Dad was—is—a control freak."

Finding she wanted to go on, wanted to tell him what she'd never told anyone, she said, "Vince was into control, too. You'd think I would have noticed, considering Dad, but I didn't. I moved in with Vince my second semester—a tough one since I had my own assignments, plus typing papers for Vince from his notes because he was so busy. I knew law school was difficult and I was eager to help. We seldom went anywhere—going places would be for later, he said.''

"Admirable character, Vince.'' David's voice held contempt.

"Definitely. I didn't catch on until spring break when plans I thought we'd made came crashing down. His excuse was an assignment by one of his profs that would take him the entire break to complete. He'd be gone most of the time, but meanwhile I could help out by getting him caught up on some overdue papers during break. When I called my parents to let them know I meant to stay on at the college, my father had a fit. So I figured I'd go home for a few days, then come back and do Vince's papers.

"What happened was that my mother got sick while I was home so I stayed longer than I intended to. I couldn't get hold of Vince to let him know, so my return went without notice. You can guess the rest. What had been keeping him so blasted 'busy' was there in bed with him. She was a grad student. At the time I hated her as much as him, but later I realized he was probably using her, too.''

"So you left both Vince and pre-law and switched to psych.''

She sighed. "While I did learn to spot users and control freaks, I soon discovered they're all over, not confined to law students and fathers.''

"I never figured I was either,'' he said.

"You're not, but you're a man and therefore suspect."

"Still?" he said, kissing her again.

"You could try to convince me otherwise," she teased, sliding her hand down his abdomen until she encountered firm evidence of arousal.

"I thought you'd never ask," he told her.

When he woke in the morning, the first thing David saw was Amy's face, beautiful as ever in sleep. He smiled, aware he'd never before spent a night like the one with her. This was what the chemistry between them had been leading up to all along. She was the sexiest partner a man could ever want.

Because she'd arranged for the sailboat to be available, he knew that sometime between the powwow Saturday night and yesterday, she'd made up her mind that their coming together was inevitable. The result was that the right time and the right place couldn't have been more perfect. He'd never forget dancing on the deck under the moon, or what came afterward. He anticipated many more nights with Amy.

Remembering the moon made him recall the words she'd murmured just before they both finally fell asleep. "Moon love," he thought she'd said, but he'd drifted off before he could ask what she'd meant.

She stirred in her sleep and he leaned to brush his lips over hers. Her eyes opened, then she gazed at him and smiled. Thinking about last night had aroused him, he didn't need any more encouragement.

She felt so good, so right against him, flesh to flesh.

Kissing her, caressing her drove him up. Her tiny moans and the way she pressed closer told him she was on the way up, too. How could he still want a woman so much when they'd spent half the night locked in each other's arms? It'd be damn difficult for him to get enough of Amy.

Maybe you never will, something inside him whispered.

He dismissed the inner voice. Never was a long, long time. Now was now and she was in his arms, and for the moment, nothing else mattered.

Afterward, all he could think was that each time they came together was like the first, with that extra edge Amy brought.

"Your turn to take us back to Incline Village," he told her near noon. Hoisting the sails, he regretted having to go back, to return to reality. This caused him to realize he hadn't given a thought to his daughter since they'd left her with Amy's brother and his wife.

"I hope Sarah wasn't upset about us not getting back last night," he said.

"She said it was okay," Amy reminded him.

"But she didn't know—"

Amy cut him off. "I told her ahead of time we might not be back until some time on Sunday. That's why her pj's and toothbrush, sleep pal and a change of clothes were in the little bag she and I packed. I said if she didn't like the idea once she met Russ and Mari and Elias, she could let me know and we'd change our plans. That's what I went over and asked her, while she was riding the pony, if she was comfortable with the idea of staying with them over-night.''

Though somewhat taken aback with how carefully Amy had planned this, he recalled Sarah's parting words—''Have fun, Daddy''—and understood Amy hadn't only been thinking of them, but of Sarah, too. Which was more than he had done until this morning. So much for his vow to protect his daughter, he told himself ruefully.

''Sarah's gained so much self-confidence since she's been with you,'' Amy continued, ''that I thought she could handle staying overnight with my brother's family. I hope I wasn't wrong.''

Still rattled by what he regarded as his own failure, he said, ''I hope so, too.''

Not until they were well under way, sails billowing in the breeze, did he realize Amy's continuing silence might mean she felt his words had been a criticism. He then realized they had been, in a way. Because she'd been more concerned about Sarah's welfare than he had.

Trying to think of another subject, anything else, he remembered her murmured words last night. ''Moon love,'' he said. ''What did you mean?''

She glanced at him. ''It's the name of one of those old songs on that CD.''

''And?''

Frowning, she looked away and said, ''Sometimes I think lawyers pry more than shrinks.''

''Only to get at the truth.''

''Why don't I believe that?''

''You're prejudiced against lawyers. And you still

haven't answered my question fully. Those two words were the last you said to me before we fell asleep.''

"Maybe the moon does affect us more than we realize. A full moon has always been associated with romance.''

"Not to mention werewolves.''

"Werewolves? What a strange thing to bring up. What made you think of…?''

"No shrinking here, Doc. You're dodging the question of what *you* meant by those words.''

She turned her head to look him straight in the eye. "Moon love isn't real love, is it? Moon love is something brought on by chemistry plus a romantic situation.''

He digested this as he trimmed the sails a bit. "So you're saying last night was moon love,'' he said when he was done.

"Wasn't it?''

What the hell kind of answer did she expect from him? Even using the word *love* made him uncomfortable. Love, the way she used it—real love—meant forever, at least that's what he understood it to mean. Forever wasn't something he could deal with. Hell, he hadn't even made up his mind what to do for a living or, actually, where he wanted to live more or less permanently. Forever was so far off in the future it was out of sight. Last night was chemistry, yes. Romantic, yes. Real love—no. Moon love? He shook his head, not liking the words applied to last night, though he couldn't explain why.

"Call it what you want,'' he muttered.

For the rest of the crossing, no comments were exchanged other than about the great weather, the beauty of the surroundings, or requests from him to help with the boat. Once docked in Haskell's marina slip, they worked together returning the sailboat to the way they found it.

"I wonder if I should clean out the refrigerator?" she said when they were finished, then answered her own question. "No, his housekeeper must take care of that."

David nodded. "I left a note thanking Mr. Haskell for the use of the *Frivolous.* Ready?"

On the drive down the mountain to her brother's ranch, Amy either dozed or pretended to. Once there, they collected Sarah, he told the Simons how grateful he was they'd taken care of his daughter overnight, and the three of them piled into the pickup. Sarah hung out the window to tell Elias she was going to invite him to ride a camel with her some time and then they were off.

Fortunately Sarah chattered all the way home about the fun she'd had at the ranch, because he had the feeling Amy and he would have had little to say to each other. How had things deteriorated so much from last night's high?

It seemed a real anticlimax to pull into Tourmaline and, at the same time, a relief. Amy would go to her own apartment and Sarah would be eager to play with her kitten, leaving him the time he needed to himself to sort through his mind's confusion.

The sight of the white Mercedes in the parking lot didn't register, not until Sarah cried, "That's *his* car," and burst into tears.

He parked the pickup and tried to calm Sarah down, but she sobbed harder. Finally Amy said, "Why don't I bring her with me while you talk to them?"

Since Sarah immediately began to cling to Amy, David decided to go along with that plan. He saw the two of them to Amy's door and then went back down the steps to deal with Iris and Murdock, who were now walking toward him.

"I know we should have phoned ahead," Iris told him, "since we originally weren't going to be here for another week." She laid a hand on Murdock's arm. "He's such a naughty boy, he drives way too fast and we forgot to call."

"That Mercedes," Murdock said. "Just can't keep her throttled down."

"Sarah's upset that you didn't let us know," David said bluntly. "She started crying so hard that Amy took her upstairs to get her calmed down."

Iris raised her eyebrows. "Well, she knew we'd be back sometime."

"Why don't we go to my apartment," he said.

Iris glanced at Murdock. "We'll go get a bite to eat somewhere," he told David. "That'll give you a chance to get the girl's things together."

"What a good idea," Iris said. "Say an hour or so?"

Watching them walk away, David clenched his fists as Murdock's "the girl's things" echoed in his head. Couldn't the creep even call Sarah by name?

Turning, he ran up the steps to Amy's apartment. As soon as Amy let him in, Sarah flew into his arms.

"Daddy, don't make me go with him," she begged, fresh tears starting. "He's going to send me away to someplace he calls a boarding school. I heard him talking to Mommy about it and she said it was a good idea. I want to stay with you and Amy."

David looked over Sarah's head at Amy, who seemed as appalled as he was, to judge by her expression.

"No," he muttered.

Sarah pulled away to stare up at him piteously. "You mean I can't stay here?"

"That's not what I meant," he assured her. His no had been an involuntary exclamation, meaning Sarah would be sent off to boarding school over his dead body.

"Your father is going to talk to your mother and stepfather before you go anywhere," Amy said.

His heart lifted just a little as he realized Amy knew how he felt.

"Mommy says I can't hate *him* because hating is bad. But I do."

"Hating hurts the one who hates," Amy told her.

"I don't have to like him." Sarah's voice was defiant.

"No, you don't," David told her. The way he felt about Murdock, he couldn't bring himself to tell her she should try to like him.

"Is he out there?" Sarah asked.

"He and your mother went to eat at a restaurant."

"He's coming back, though, isn't he?" Sarah's lip began to quiver.

"How about some coffee for us and chocolate milk

for Sarah while we wait?'' Amy asked. "I'll make the coffee and Sarah can stir the chocolate syrup into her milk.''

"Go ahead,'' he told Amy. "I'm going to make a phone call.''

Taking Amy's phone into the living room, he called Gert and explained the problem. "You're an old friend of Judge Maguire's,'' he said. "Considering it's Sunday, what are the chances he'd take it in stride if you called him at home right now?''

He listened, nodding. "Good.'' He explained the problem ending with, "I want you to ask him if I can get a temporary injunction tomorrow to keep Sarah here since I believe—and it's also Amy's professional opinion—that it would do my daughter real harm to be shipped off to boarding school while she's in therapy for emotional problems.''

When he returned to the kitchen, the coffee was brewing and Sarah was concentrating on pouring the right amount of syrup into a glass of milk. He waited until she'd finished and was stirring the mixture with a spoon.

"You won't be going anywhere tonight, Sarah, except home to sleep in your own bed.''

Her face brightened. "You mean I can stay with you?''

"Tonight for sure. What happens after that hasn't been settled yet.''

"Oh.'' She sighed.

"Your father is going to do his best for you,'' Amy said.

"You mean it's like maybe?''

When Amy nodded, Sarah smiled. "When Daddy says maybe he usually means yes."

When he finished his coffee, David left Sarah with Amy and went to his own apartment. Hobo greeted him by twining between his ankles and he had to look down to be sure he didn't step on any of the kittens.

He gathered all of them up and shut them, with their mother, in his bedroom. No way did he intend to have anyone distracted by kittens climbing all over them. While he waited for Iris and Murdock, he marshaled his thoughts, setting them in clear order as though for a court case. Which it well might turn out to be.

By the time the Murdocks showed up at his door, David's anger had cooled from white-hot rage to a cold determination. He invited them to be seated, but brushed off any small talk. "I want you both to understand that I am not going to allow my daughter to be sent away to a boarding school," he said.

"Not allow?" Iris cried. "Since when have you taken any interest in her schooling?"

"I haven't interfered until now," he continued, ignoring her remarks, "because I supposed Sarah was better off with her mother. I discovered I was mistaken."

Iris glared at him. "Are you accusing me of—?"

He interrupted her. "I'm not accusing you of anything. I'm stating that, as her father, I believe sending Sarah to boarding school would be harmful to her improvement. She is receiving required therapy, you know."

"Is that so?" Murdock huffed. "Required for what?"

David wasn't giving an inch. "You'll have to speak to her psychologist if you need to know about Sarah's progress. We can settle this here and now or you can wait for me to get a temporary restraining order from Judge Maguire in the morning, ordering you to refrain from moving my daughter until the court determines the state of her mental health."

Iris stood up. "Where is Sarah? I demand to see her right now." She glanced at Murdock. "Brent, make him let me talk to her."

"You certainly can see Sarah, Iris," David said. "But not until we settle this problem."

"I demand—" she began, her voice rising.

"Be quiet, Iris," Murdock snapped. "If you can't stay calm, go sit in the car and let me handle things."

She glared at him, but shut up and sat down.

Focusing on Murdock, David said, "At present, Iris and I have joint custody. I was shocked to discover, when you dropped her off here with me, that Sarah was so desperately insecure I had to arrange for psychological counseling. Now I find you intend to ship this insecure little girl off to a boarding school. What other recourse do I have but to sue for full custody?"

"You wouldn't dare do that," Iris said. "Not after what happened in Albuquerque. A judge would never—"

"Iris, I told you to keep quiet or leave us." Murdock's voice was as cold as David had ever heard it.

"I don't mind digging up the past," David said. "I don't believe I ever told you about the letter I got from that juror who changed his story. After I moved here, he also sent me a clipping from the *Journal* about your wedding." He stared straight at Murdock. "If I have to resurrect the entire dirty mess, I will, make no mistake."

Murdock blinked, making David aware he'd gotten to him. "Naturally," he added, "Sarah could visit you two whenever it's convenient for all concerned. I assume you intend to travel a lot or you wouldn't have considered boarding school."

Iris's gaze flicked from Murdock to David and back, but she said nothing.

Looking at Iris, but speaking, David knew, to him, Murdock said, "My dear, you must admit David has a point here. Perhaps Sarah would be better off with him having full custody. He's willing to allow her to visit and that can be written into the agreement. I really dislike the idea of disrupting the child's therapy. We'd be at fault if anything went wrong."

David decided this was the moment to leave them alone to settle things between them. "Fine. I'm glad we agree this should be resolved amicably. I'll bring Sarah home now so that she'll have a chance to see her mother." Without waiting for a reply, he rose, crossed to the door and went out.

Outside, he released a long breath of relief. As soon as he'd realized Murdock called the shots, not Iris, he'd been pretty sure a not-so-veiled threat would avoid any wrangling in court over custody. The last thing Murdock would want was any probing into that juror affair. His bluff had worked.

When he ushered Sarah into his apartment after assuring her she'd be staying with him, she clung tightly to his hand, not even letting go when Iris flung herself to her knees beside Sarah and hugged her.

"Are you sure you want to stay with your father?" Iris asked her.

Sarah nodded.

"You can come home with Mommy, if you want to."

"No," Sarah said, loud and clear.

Iris pulled away from her and rose to her feet, looking distressed.

"I'll come and visit you sometime, Mommy," Sarah said, her words easing her mother's stricken look.

Iris looked at David, "See that she does."

"Definitely," he told her. "When it's convenient all around."

Sarah hadn't so much as glanced at Murdock. When he came up to stand beside her mother, he said, "Aren't you going to say goodbye to me?"

"Bye," Sarah said, still not looking at him.

Iris bent and kissed her. "Goodbye, my darling," she said.

"Bye, Mommy." She didn't let go of David's hand until the door closed behind them.

"I might miss Mommy, sometimes," she admitted then, "but I won't miss *him.* You won't ever send me to boarding school, will you, Daddy?"

"Never."

"Now we have to go tell Amy. She'll be happy I get to stay with you, 'cause she likes me." Sarah paused a moment. "I like her a whole lot. You like Amy, too, don't you?"

"You bet," he told his daughter. Among other things, he added to himself. The problem was some of those other things scared the hell out of him.

Chapter Eleven

Amy could hardly wait to get home on Monday afternoon. Though David had told her Sarah was going to stay with him, she was eager to find out the details. She found the two of them in the play area of the complex, David throwing a ball for Sarah to bat. Amy tried to ignore the flutter in her stomach at the sight of David.

"I'm learning to play baseball," Sarah informed her.

"So I see. My brother taught me when I was a girl, but I never was a good batter."

"Daddy says I'm improving." As usual when she'd just learned a new word, Sarah pronounced it carefully. "It means I'm getting better." She put down her bat. "I wish I had a brother."

David raised his eyebrows. "You'll have to be satisfied with your kitten, punkin."

"That's *calabaza,*" Sarah informed him with a giggle. "My violin teacher taught us to count in Spanish, so I asked her if she knew how to say pumpkin in Spanish and she did."

Sarah turned to Amy. "Betty's having a birthday party and I'm invited. Betty's mother's taking me and two other girls to McDonald's. I got Betty a toy kitten 'cause she likes Sheba so much, but she can't have any pets where she lives. Pretty soon it'll be my birthday and I'm going to have a party, too. You're invited."

Amy smiled at her. "I wouldn't miss it for the world."

A honk caught Sarah's attention. "That's Betty's mother." She grabbed a colorful bag from the nearby picnic table, said a hasty goodbye and ran toward the van.

"When is her birthday?" Amy asked David.

"This Friday, but we're going to wait until Saturday so you and Gert can come."

"To McDonald's?"

"Not. Gert offered her backyard so this'll be an outdoor affair."

"Al fresco. Sounds like fun."

"I'm relying on you to help me make it a little girl's party. The ones I went to as a kid were mostly the boy kind."

"Sure." Amy did her best to hide her pleasure. "I'm so glad you persuaded the Murdocks to leave

Sarah here with you. I've never seen her so frightened.''

David scowled. "*Threatened* Murdock comes closer to the mark. I filed for sole custody of Sarah today.''

"You did? Wonderful. Do you think they'll fight it?''

He shook his head. "He agreed after I told him I meant to fight dirty if I had to. Iris—'' he paused. "We agreed Sarah will be able to visit her mother whenever it's convenient for everyone.''

Amy couldn't imagine herself agreeing to give up a child to the extent Iris would be giving up Sarah. Not that she planned on having children. Though a single parent could raise a well-adjusted child, children profited by having both a mother and a father raising them. Marriage was the best arrangement for that, but she didn't have any intention of tying herself to any man and allowing him to control her.

She was pleased for David, though—he really loved his daughter. Amy thought it significant that he'd so quickly used the law to protect Sarah. It persuaded her she'd been right all along. He'd been in denial, refusing to face the fact that being a lawyer was what he really wanted to do, despite what had happened in New Mexico. She opened her mouth to say something of the sort, but he spoke first.

"Your place or mine?''

Her breath caught. Looking at him from under her lashes, she said, "For dinner, you mean?''

"That, too.''

The glow deep in those blue, blue eyes of his speeded her pulse. "Leftovers," she managed to say.

"Not enough."

She slanted him a look. "I guess you must be hungry."

"Understatement of the year. If we don't get under cover fast, you can't hold me accountable." He grabbed her hand, pulling her with him. "Your place is closer."

By the time they reached the top of the stairs she was breathless, and not from the climb. He hadn't yet kissed her, but already anticipatory heat pooled low inside her.

As soon as David kicked the door shut behind them, he reached for Amy, holding her away from him for a moment, seeing his own need reflected in her eyes. "We're never going to make it to the bedroom," he murmured, pulling her close and slanting his mouth over hers.

He breathed in her arousing floral scent, the taste of her more intoxicating than wine. She returned his kiss with passion, letting him know she wanted more. Like he did. Would he ever have enough of Amy?

Her hair, soft and silken, brushed his cheek, reminding him that her skin under all those clothes was even softer. It seemed forever since they'd lain together flesh to flesh; he couldn't wait to hold her that way again.

Shedding clothes as they paused en route to the bedroom for just one more kiss, then another and another, they finally reached the bed naked. With more control than he'd known he possessed, he resisted the urge to plunge into her warm, welcoming depths. Sex with Amy was more than scratching an itch, he wanted to savor every second along the way. Actually, sex wasn't the right word. Lovemaking?

"You're so beautiful," he whispered in her ear as he caressed her breasts before nibbling at them. And she was, every part of her.

"So are you," she murmured, holding him close.

No one had ever called him beautiful before. He didn't believe he was, but it touched his heart that she thought so. A feeling of tenderness swept through him, different from the heat of desire rising with every pulse beat. He needed Amy in a way he'd never needed any other woman.

Her gasping moans, her pleas of "Now, now," drove him wild until he lost control and joined with her, everything a blur except sensation. Even in his daze of passion, though, he knew she was with him all the way to the top and over. Afterward he was reluctant to let her go. Only the possibility that Sarah might return kept him from beginning all over again. Once was far from enough.

"You're addictive," he murmured.

"I was just thinking the same thing about you."

"Who was it advised moderation in all things?"

"Some holy man, maybe."

He nodded. "Easy for them to say when they weren't holding the sexiest woman in the world in their arms."

Her smile was lazy, satisfied. Because of him. Because of the fire that blazed out of control when they touched each other. He wanted to tell her—what? He couldn't find words that expressed what he meant. He wasn't even sure he knew what it was. He finally said, "That was no rewarmed leftover. I'd call it prime gourmet."

"Still hungry?"

He bent to kiss her, murmuring, "What do you think?"

She responded with interest, but after several moments pulled away. "When is Sarah due back?"

He sighed. "I figure it's time to shift base to my apartment." As they collected their strewn clothes, he asked, "Back to leftovers. What kind?"

"We're talking food now, right? Some deli roast beef, a few slices of cheese, baby carrots, maybe a tomato. Yogurt."

"Combined with my half loaf of rye, some aging lettuce, grapes and Popsicles, we have the makings of a gourmet feast."

"You like Popsicles?"

"Never got over them."

"Me, neither. You go ahead. I'll bring my stuff to your place in a bit."

Amy watched David leave, admiring the easy way he moved, basking in the intimate smile he gave her on the way out. She shook her head. If she didn't watch herself, she was apt to turn into a David groupie and that would never do.

You are an independent woman, she told herself firmly. Never lose sight of that. Otherwise it'll be all too easy to find yourself being controlled by a man once again.

She grimaced. As a psychologist, she understood

she was stereotyping all men as controlling—which was wrong. But as a woman, she found it difficult not to. Physician, heal thyself? Not that easy.

That didn't mean she couldn't enjoy making love with David, she just had to remember it was only chemistry. Except *only* was too wimpy a word to describe what happened between them when he kissed her.

And imagine that—a man who not only liked Popsicles, but admitted he did. Who'd have thought it? Her favorite flavor was grape. She wondered what his might be. Before she knew it she'd slipped into a reverie about sharing a grape Popsicle with him while they made love. With an effort she snapped back into reality and headed for the refrigerator to gather her leftovers.

Saturday Amy headed over to Gert's early to help her get ready for Sarah's birthday party. Betty's mother, Cary, had offered to pitch in, too, but then had called to say she was ill and couldn't. She'd sounded so bad that Amy stopped by to see her on the way.

"I'll be okay," a pale and shaky Cary told her. "It's just my darn gallbladder acting up again. I hope I won't need surgery. Especially since—" She broke off, then added, "I suppose it's never a good time to have surgery, is it?"

"I'll pick up Betty for Sarah's party and bring her back," Amy said. "Is there anything else I can do for you?"

Cary sighed. "Thanks. I'll manage."

As she drove away, Amy hoped Cary was right about being able to manage. Perhaps when she picked up Betty she'd ask if the girl could spend the night with Sarah. At her place, since she was sure David had no idea how much little girls could giggle at a slumber party.

Gert thought it was a good idea. "It'll be an extra present for Sarah, plus helping out Betty's mother. Weren't you and David planning to take Sarah on Sunday to see the moving stones at the Carson Sink? You might want to take in the Fallon Air Show as well. Betty could go, too."

"I'll mention that to Cary."

The party, with two other girls from the violin class besides Betty, was a smashing success. "The best one I ever had," Sarah told Amy and David later on the front porch. "Mostly Mommy took me out for lunch on my birthday and then we went shopping. This was more fun."

David winced inwardly, aware he hadn't paid much attention to Sarah's birthdays for the past few years other than buying her a present. "I hear the fun's not over yet," he said. "You and Betty and Amy are having a slumber party."

"I'm sorry you can't come, Daddy, but boys aren't allowed." Sarah turned to Betty. "Come on, we'll go in and ask Great-aunt Gert if I can show you that ballerina music box I told you about."

As the two little girls disappeared inside, David and Amy looked at each other, shaking their heads. Remembering how upset Sarah had been when she first saw the music box, he said, "She's changed a lot—all good. Thanks to you."

"I just gave advice—you took it. That's what's made the change."

"Not all of it. We—" He paused. Had he been about to say the three of them were like a family? Some truth to that, but better left unsaid.

Amy raised an eyebrow when he didn't continue, finally shrugging. "Gert mentioned the air show at Fallon tomorrow. Are you up for it?" she asked.

He leaned close and murmured, "Want to guess what I'd rather be up for?"

To his delight, Amy blushed.

"Good grief, you'd think I was sixteen," she muttered.

He leaned closer still, his lips brushing hers, when he heard a truck pull into the drive. Damn.

The truck stopped. "Don't let me disturb you," Grandfather said as he climbed down from the pickup.

"There you are." Gert's voice came from the vestibule leading to the porch. She pushed open the screen and waved at Grandfather. "Care for some limeade before we go?"

He nodded as he climbed the stairs, and she waved him to a seat. "Sarah's party over?" he asked, holding up a hide bag drawn together with a thong. "I brought her a talisman."

"I'll tell her you're here," Gert said, and went in.

Grandfather looked from Amy to David and back, his dark eyes gleaming. "Hawks mate for life."

Jolted, David involuntarily glanced at Amy. She looked as surprised as he felt.

"Just so you know," Grandfather added with a grin.

Before either of them recovered enough to say anything, Sarah burst through the screen door, Betty behind her. "Hi, Grandfather," Sarah said. "This is my friend Betty."

"Friends are good to have," he said, motioning Sarah closer. "I brought you something for your seventh birthday."

He reached into the drawstring bag and lifted out a small carving made of a glossy brown wood. "Shane carved it for me and I carried it here in my medicine bag to give it power."

"What kind of power?" Sarah asked.

"Good medicine." He placed the carving in her hand.

Sarah gazed at it intently for long moments. Finally she smiled. "I think I can sort of feel the good medicine." She bent and kissed the old man on the cheek. "Thank you."

Betty, looking at the carving, murmured, "Awesome."

"See, Daddy," Sarah said, crossing to him.

He studied the intricate carving. Two hawks, each feather carefully delineated, perched on the limb of a tree, one with wings outspread as though just landing, the other with closed wings.

Amy leaned toward him to peer at the hawks.

"Together," Grandfather said. "I dream true."

A silence fell. From somewhere in the distance,

David heard the faint cry of a hunting hawk. He searched the sky but didn't see the bird. Probably his imagination. Grandfather had a way of unsettling people.

Gert came out onto the porch with the limeade pitcher and glasses and the moment dissipated.

"Look what Grandfather gave me," Sarah said to Gert. "Sage's father made it."

"Beautiful work," Gert told her. "A wonderful talisman. That word means it brings good fortune, Sarah."

"Like good luck?" Betty asked.

"Exactly."

Betty sighed. "I wish—" She broke off, lowering her head, but not before David saw guilt shadow her face.

Amy put an arm around Betty's shoulders, murmuring, "We all wish for good luck."

Her response to Betty warmed him. Sure, she was a psychologist, but he knew her well enough by now to understand it was Amy consoling the girl, not Dr. Simon.

"If no one else wants limeade," Gert said, "I'm going to put away the pitcher and get ready to go to Walker Lake."

Sarah smiled at her. "Have fun," she said.

Gert nodded. "Fun is a good thing to look forward to. We all need to remember that."

Sarah had said the same thing to him when he and Amy went sailing the previous Saturday. He smiled, remembering. He and Frivolous Amy did have fun— and one hell of a lot more.

Unfortunately, he didn't see any way to get Amy alone tonight, what with the slumber party going on. Sunday Betty would still be with them, at least until they returned from Fallon and dropped her off at home. Even then, there was no one to leave Sarah with since who knew when Gert would get back.

He loved his daughter and wouldn't give her up for the world, but he had to admit carrying on an affair was a damn sight easier for an unencumbered man.

Inspiration struck. There wouldn't be time for more than holding and kissing Amy, but something was better than nothing. He hurried after Gert, who had gone into the house.

"Okay if Amy and I look for something in the attic before you leave?" he asked her.

Gert smiled slightly. "Go ahead. You've got maybe ten minutes." The trouble with having a shrink for a relative was that she always saw through your cover story, he thought as he went to collect Amy.

As they climbed the attic stairs, she asked, "What is it we're looking for?"

"I'll know it when I see it," he assured her.

"That's not a lot of help."

"Maybe not, but it's the truth." He waited until she reached the top, then pulled her into his arms. "Found it already," he murmured as he bent to kiss her.

"You're so bad," she whispered against his lips as they covered hers.

Instant fire ran through his veins when she opened to him, her hands caressing his nape, her softness pressing close against him. Every time he touched her, she responded, her eagerness inflaming him, because it meant her desire matched his. He tried to control the wild flare of need consuming him. Ten minutes? Not time enough to make love with her the way he wanted to. Ten hours, maybe. Ten days. Ten years?

Ten years? The words roiled in his mind. A long time. Long enough? How could he tell when all he knew right now was that he'd have one hell of a time doing without Amy.

She felt so right against him, as though no other woman would ever fit quite so well.

He explored the hollow of her throat where her pulse beat rapidly against his lips, matching the racing of his own heart.

"We can't," she whispered. "Not here."

He knew she was right, but he couldn't let her go, not yet. Not ever, the way he felt at the moment. Cupping her bottom, he raised her up and rocked her against his arousal, catching her gasp of need in his mouth as he kissed her again, hard and deep and long.

Stop, he warned himself, or you'll go over the edge and take her on this damn, dusty attic floor.

When he finally made himself release her, she stepped sideways, bracing herself against the wall. He watched her catch her breath, then look at him with those sea-green eyes of hers. "Like Emerald Bay," he rasped.

"Not quite." Her voice wasn't completely steady. "Your eyes, I mean."

"I've never put a name to the color of yours. Cerulean, like the sky? Or maybe indigo blue? Or something in between that's unique. Matchless.'' She put a hand to her mouth. "Heavens, I'm babbling."

He cleared his throat to rid himself of the passion-induced hoarseness. "I rather like being matchless."

"I was only referring to your eyes."

The tartness in her voice amused him, taking him back to their first meeting. Though she'd annoyed him, he'd liked her even then.

"You brought me up here to seduce me," she accused.

"Spot on." He grinned at her. "I'll have to confess to Gert that I didn't quite locate what I was looking for in the attic."

"Don't you dare." She glanced around at the attic clutter. "We'll find something."

He didn't tell her Gert knew perfectly well why he'd hauled Amy up here.

"Look," she said. "Over there." She gestured toward an old bureau. Atop it sat a large orange pumpkin.

He nodded. Sarah would love it. He bulldozed his way among boxes and old furniture to reach the bureau. The pumpkin, he saw, wasn't plastic, as he'd expected, but ceramic, with a lid. He lifted the lid and peered inside. "Marbles," he said. "It's half full of marbles. I haven't seen any since I stayed with Grandpa. He taught me how to shoot marbles. Just wait until I show Sarah how to play."

"My brother taught me," Amy said. "I used to be pretty good."

"Is that a challenge?"

"Why not?"

"I accept. Winner gets to finish what we started up here."

She made a face at him but didn't disagree.

He carried the pumpkin down to the porch where Gert told him it came with the house. "Like most of that attic clutter. So you're welcome to it, marbles and all."

A very good day, all things considered, he thought as he drove home with his find. The girls had elected to go with Amy, so he was alone. Could have been better in one way. Still, as Amy had insisted on the boat, anticipation made the heart grow fonder. Or something of the sort.

Fondness wasn't quite the right word for how he felt about her. Nor affection. And, though he did like her, there was more to it. The word *love* hovered on the brink of his thoughts, but he shook his head. He loved his daughter, yes. Parent love. And his sister Diane. Family love.

He sincerely doubted that he'd ever loved Iris. Lusted for her at one time, yes. And look at the trouble that had gotten him into. She obviously had never really loved him, either. She'd thought he represented security and eventual wealth, but discovered she could bypass the eventual by attracting a man who already had the money she craved, plus the time to help her spend it.

Amy wasn't like that. He smiled, thinking the word for her was one she'd used about his eyes. Whether they were matchless or not, she certainly was. Love, though, was pushing the envelope.

Chapter Twelve

Sunday dawned fair and warm, but, by the time the four of them were ready to set off on their excursion, a thin haze dulled the blue of the sky and the day grew hot. The high desert made it a dry heat, but hot was hot. When they reached the Carson Sink area, they'd finished all the bottled water despite the truck's air-conditioning.

"There's hardly even any sagebrush out here," Betty commented.

Amy, looking at the bleak, arid landscape, thought she'd never seen such a desolate spot.

"Why doesn't the Carson River keep going instead of sinking into the sand out here?" Sarah asked.

"All the rivers in the area do the same thing," David said. "They run out of enough water to keep flowing. What's left eventually sinks into the sand."

"Is this where the rocks move all by themselves?" Sarah said after they parked and got out.

"They get some help from the winds," David said.

The hot wind hit Amy like a blast from a steel mill furnace. "How big are these so-called walking rocks?" she asked.

He pointed to the flat ahead of them where rocks resembling partially squashed melons were scattered. Underfoot the sand felt dry, though out farther it looked somewhat darker, as though it might be damp. When they neared the first rock, Amy saw what she thought was a snake track.

"See the trail this one left when the wind blew it?" David asked.

"Do we get to see them move?" Sarah asked.

"No, we'd have to stand here for hours, maybe days to do that. But you can see where they started from and where they are now."

Amy discarded the notion of snake tracks when she saw that all the rocks in their immediate vicinity had left similar squiggly trails. "How hard does the wind have to blow—like a hurricane?"

He shook his head. "The sun dries the topmost sand, but underneath is mud from the water continually sinking in. This dampness allows the wind, constant out here, to move the rocks millimeter by millimeter—" he held up his thumb and forefinger to show the tiny distance "—night and day until they finally leave a trail we can see."

"It'd be more fun it we got to watch it," Betty said.

Amy had to admit she was right. Not only was the

area desolate, but the vision of the river ending like this depressed her. Water should flow grandly into the sea, a lake or a larger river, not just give up and sink into the ground.

"I can't argue with that," David said. "Let's go. I guarantee the air show'll be more fun."

He was right, even though they had to walk what seemed like miles from where the parking area was to where a lot of planes were parked on the tarmac. Amy had thought it hot before, but once she stepped onto the tarmac, the heat overwhelmed her.

"It's 105," a man passing told his companion.

"Is that degrees?" she asked David.

"Feels about that, yeah."

"I'm thirsty, Daddy, and so is Betty," Sarah said plaintively.

They detoured to the vendor stand for soft drinks.

"People are climbing inside that great big plane," Sarah said when they finished the drinks. "Can we go?"

Consulting the flyer he'd gotten at the gate, David said, "That's a C5-A, a military transport plane."

Whatever it was, the plane was huge. As she climbed the steps, Amy felt she was entering the belly of a whale. Once they were inside, though, she was bathed in blessed coolness. Sighing, she sat down on a long bench that ran along one side of the plane's belly.

"Let's imagine we're sailors who've been swallowed by a whale," she said to Sarah and Betty.

"Awesome," Betty said.

"Except it'd have to be a whale made out of—" Sarah hesitated, obviously stuck for the right word.

"A robot whale," David said.

Sarah nodded. "So if we had the controls we could get out."

Amy was constantly amazed at how much children knew at an early age. Had she understood what a robot was when she was seven? She couldn't remember. She was listening to the girls jabbering back and forth, making up a story about the robot whale, when her gaze met David's over their heads.

If she read that look correctly, he was wishing the two of them were alone together elsewhere. What, she wondered, did he see in her eyes? Was he remembering the night in Emerald Bay? She'd gone over that night so many times in her mind, reliving every word, every kiss, every caress.

She couldn't be sure what she felt for David. Was it only moon love? Or was it more, an emotion she was afraid to recognize?

A roar from the crowd outside brought her back to the belly of the C5-A. A louder jet roar drowned out the noise from the crowd.

"Show's starting," David said. "Up and out."

"Is that like over and out?" Betty asked. "They say that a lot on TV."

"He means it's time to go out and watch what's happening in the air," Amy said.

Finding it cool in the shade of the transport's huge wings, at least as compared to being in the sun, Amy refused to move on. "We can see fine from here."

The amazing feats of the newest navy fighters as

they zoomed through the sky, sometimes flying straight up at what seemed like an impossible speed, held her in thrall.

"A tad faster than a sailplane," David said into Amy's ear, his breath tickling her, sending tingling squiggles along her nerve endings. "Noisier, too."

Halfway through the precision performance of the Blue Angels, Sarah tugged at Amy's hand. Unable to hear her over the noise, Amy crouched down to her level.

"Can we go?" Sarah asked. "I told Daddy I was tired, but he didn't hear me."

"Right away." Amy looked at David, his rapt gaze on the navy jets. He didn't seem to hear her when she called his name, so she reached up and tugged at his earlobe.

He started, then turned to her.

"The girls are worn-out," she half shouted.

He nodded. Then, without a word of protest, he took each girl by the hand and headed for the car.

A good guy, Amy told herself as she brought up the rear. A good father. And a fantastic lover. Like most men, he was into control, but, admit it, not unbearably so. She couldn't imagine him behaving the way Vince had. David was different. He was, like his eyes, matchless. What made her so afraid of admitting what she really felt? Saying past experience was a cop-out. Everyone had to grow and change or stagnate.

Okay, so love had crept up on her, taking her by surprise. She certainly hadn't meant for it to happen. She wondered what David would do if she all of a sudden blurted out that she loved him. After his experience with Iris, run, probably. In any case, she didn't intend to so much as give him a clue about how she felt.

By the time they reached Tourmaline, both girls were asleep in the back seat of the cab. Betty woke when David unfastened her seat belt and she stumbled sleepily along beside him to her mother's door.

"Cary says she's feeling better," he reported when he returned to the truck. "Plans to go to work tomorrow."

"I'm glad," Amy said.

At the apartment complex, he couldn't rouse Sarah enough to walk so he tossed his keys to Amy so she could unlock the door, then carried his daughter inside and laid her on her bed. Amy took off Sarah's shoes, but since it wasn't even dark yet, left her dressed, pulling a light quilt over her.

"I think she'll wake up before long," she told David. "Probably hungry."

Back in the kitchen, he said, "I'll call in a pizza order so you and I can eat and there'll be leftovers for Sarah."

By the time the pizza arrived, the kittens had discovered they were home and Amy had two of them climbing all over her.

"They must think I'm a tree," she said as one of the black-and-white ones, on her shoulder, started licking her ear.

She returned both kittens to the floor, washed her hands and got out plates, glasses and napkins while David cut the pizza. A tranquil domestic scene, she thought. A family scene. Though she'd never pictured herself as particularly domestic, somehow it seemed so right.

"Have you heard from Cal?" she asked as they sat down to eat.

David nodded. "He told me Dodie Thomas came through for him. She went down to the sheriff's office and gave a statement about the accident that lets Cal off the hook and puts the blame where it belongs."

"Will you have to go to court?"

"Depends on whether those dipsticks cop a plea."

Which meant he would if Cal needed him to. "I suppose this is pro bono work," she said.

"Cal offered to pay me. I told him if he got a good insurance settlement, okay, otherwise I wouldn't charge him."

Chances were the van was insured and so Cal ought to be granted a decent-size settlement, considering the charges against the driver. Which meant David was back to being a lawyer with a paying client. A giant step in the right direction.

Elated, Amy spoke before she thought. "Bye-bye denial and good riddance. You're cured."

David blinked at her for a moment before his expression turned stony. "I thought you'd promised to stop analyzing me. I see I was wrong."

"I—I—" she stammered, realizing she'd made a mistake.

He set down his glass of root beer. "Get this straight. I do not intend to enter the practice of law again. I'll maintain my Nevada licensure strictly for emergencies. Cal's problem was in that category, just like filing for sole custody of Sarah was.'' His voice was colder than his chill gaze.

Amy searched for words to explain but could find none. While she hadn't actually promised David anything, she knew very well she'd led him to believe she'd stopped analyzing him.

"I. Am. Not. Your. Patient.'' David's clipped words left no doubt about his state of mind. "We'd agreed on that. You went back on your word. Betrayed me.''

"I—I have to go,'' Amy muttered, sliding off the stool.

"Even if I had been in denial,'' he added as she headed for the door, "you're wrong, you know.''

Those last words of his stayed with her as she fled from his apartment. *Wrong.* Yes, she'd been wrong, in the same way she'd been wrong in the Giesau case, one that still haunted her. Her mentor had excused her because she'd just started to work with patients, but she'd never been able to excuse herself, just like she couldn't now. Had she learned nothing since that time?

She'd harmed Olivia Giesau in the past by not understanding her. Because of this, the young woman had tried to commit suicide and almost succeeded. Though it was true she hadn't harmed David here and now, she'd destroyed his trust in her and, along with it, any chance of a relationship between them. What must he think of her?

Tears trickled down her cheeks as she closed herself into her own place and locked the door. A vision of the Carson Sink flashed into her mind, making her realize her heart felt as barren as that desolate place. How could she have been so careless? Or, worse, how could she have gone on trying to push him out of denial after agreeing not to? She'd been wrong, and it served her right to be stuck with a love forever unrequited. At this thought, she burst into sobs.

Later, tears dried and face washed, Amy made up her mind not to continue feeling sorry for herself, since that was negative and nonproductive. She couldn't go back and undo the damage, but she could and would go on from here. Since living in the same apartment complex meant she'd run into David from time to time, she decided a cool but not totally unfriendly attitude was what she'd employ. She'd tuck her love for him away in the attic of her mind, and in time, she'd forget. Wouldn't she?

But what was she to do about Sarah?

David's anger, completely justified, he assured himself, had cooled to a simmer by the time Sarah woke up. But it didn't help that her first words as she straggled into the kitchen were "Where's Amy?"

"She had to go home."

Something in his voice must have given him away because Sarah gave him an odd look, though all she said was "Oh."

He served Sarah some pizza and milk, wondering how he was going to explain why they wouldn't be seeing much of Amy anymore.

Sarah polished off one slice of pizza and was working on another, when she stopped eating to say, "Are you mad at Amy?"

Since "no" would be an outright lie, he said, "Not exactly."

Sarah eyed him for a moment, then said, "I like Amy. She's my friend."

He heard the thread of defiance in his daughter's voice and realized avoiding Amy wasn't going to be as easy as he'd imagined. Sarah wouldn't understand if he cut Amy out of her life as well as his.

Instead of tackling the problem head-on, he decided he'd be better off easing Sarah out of the relationship she had with Amy. He changed the subject.

"I'm going to start building that gazebo Gert wanted in her backyard. Tomorrow you can help me pick out the lumber and then you can be my regular helper as we build it. Okay?"

"Okay, but don't forget I have to start school next week. You said you were going to register me tomorrow."

Touched as always by her careful pronunciation of the new word she'd learned, David said, "We can pick up the lumber afterward." The truth was he'd completely forgotten about the registration.

"It's the same school Betty goes to, so I already have a friend there," Sarah said. "Isn't that lucky? Do you think that's because of the talisman Grandfather gave me?"

"It never hurts to have a good-luck piece, but you knew Betty and you were at the same school before he gave you that gift."

"Yeah." She finished the second slice of pizza, took a long swallow of milk, then said, "If you want to borrow my talisman, you can."

"Do you think I need good luck?"

She nodded. "Amy said everybody wishes for good luck. So I'll put the hawks in your bedroom so you can see them every day."

Sarah meant well, so he forced himself to thank her, though the last thing he wanted to see when he went to bed at night was those two damn hawks.

He sat sipping coffee while she finished up her milk with two cookies, trying to tell himself he wasn't brooding. Why was he attracted to women who betrayed him in one way or another? Iris's betrayal was far more gross than Amy's, but it angered and hurt him to think Amy might have been thinking of him as a patient all along.

"Betty says the doctor told her mother she had to have an operation," Sarah said. "That's when you go to the hospital and get cut open, isn't it?"

"Yes. But Mrs. McBride told me last night that she felt better."

"Betty's scared."

"Well, even if her mother does have the operation, Betty's father will be there to see to things, so she'll be okay."

"Betty says he hasn't been home for a really long time."

Preoccupied with his own problem, David wasn't really concentrating on what Sarah said. "Don't worry, punkin," he told her. "If push comes to shove, I'm sure Betty's father will be there."

Sarah stared at him. "What's 'push comes to shove' mean?"

He tried to explain, realizing he was making a

botch of it when Sarah only looked more puzzled. The truth was, he wasn't running on all cylinders because of Amy. "Never mind," he said. "I'm sure Betty will be well taken care of no matter what."

"Amy said she'd shoot marbles with us when she comes home tomorrow. Why do you call it shoot?"

Rather than try to explain, he opened the pumpkin, took out a handful of marbles and gave Sarah her first lesson on the kitchen floor. Naturally the kittens thought the rolling marbles were playthings, making Sarah giggle rather than learn.

He let her take Sheba to bed with her, knowing once Sarah fell asleep, the kitten would make her way back to the box where the other kittens slept with their mother.

As he retired for the night he saw that his daughter had already transferred the hawks talisman to his dresser. He scowled at it, knowing he'd be lucky to get any sleep at all tonight.

On Monday, Gert stopped Amy as she was leaving the office for the day. "If you're not feeling well," she said, "take the day off tomorrow."

Amy sighed inwardly. It was difficult to fool Gert.

"It's just that I didn't sleep well last night," she said.

Gert's assessing gaze told her as clearly as words that she knew there was more to it than that, but all she said was "Take care of yourself."

When Amy drove into her carport, she spotted Sarah at the edge of the playground with David. Since Sarah was looking her way, she waved, then started for the stairs to her apartment. Before she reached them, Sarah ran up to her.

"You promised to shoot marbles with us," she said.

"I'm not dressed for it," Amy parried.

"We'll wait while you change."

What was she supposed to do now? Well, she'd known it wouldn't be easy. "I'm not sure I—"

"Please?" Sarah asked.

Unable to disappoint the girl, Amy gave in. "Just for a few minutes, though."

When she came back out, Sarah was once again with her father, both crouched in the dirt. Amy's pace lagged as she headed toward them. She plain wasn't ready to see David yet. She'd thrown on the first clothes that were handy and now belatedly realized she had on the beige shorts that she used for cleaning because they were really too short to wear outside. Blast it.

Dawdle as she might, she finally came up to them. "Hi," she said to David, not quite looking at him.

He nodded to her. "Got to get down and dirty here if you're serious," he said. "Here's your shooter and ten glassies." He handed her ten marbles, one slightly larger than the rest of the glassies.

She stared down at the ring drawn in the dirt with a stick.

"You have to put five of your marbles in the ring," Sarah said.

Amy dropped to her knees since, as she knew, there was no other way to play. She tried to conjure up some memory of what she'd learned about the game from her brother, but her brain wasn't functioning too well with David so close beside her.

"It seems to me Russ used to dig a hole in the dirt with his heel," she said as she dropped five of her marbles into the ring.

"That's another way to play," David agreed.

"Betty thinks it's neat your brother raises horses," Sarah said to Amy.

Amy smiled at her. "Me, too."

"Okay, as youngest, Sarah gets to shoot first," David said.

The girl carefully positioned her shooter on her thumbnail, with her forefinger keeping the marble from rolling off, then flicked her thumb, sending the marble flying into the ring where it knocked two of the smaller marbles out of the ring boundaries.

"I get to keep those," Sarah cried.

"I can see you've been practicing," Amy said.

"Daddy taught me. But he's lots better."

Then it was Amy's turn and she bent over to position her marble.

David, in back of her, wound up with an unexpected view of more of Amy's rear end than he could deal with when her shorts pulled up to reveal the soft white flesh of part of her buttocks. The sight went straight to his groin. Damn. He might be angry with her, but that sure as hell didn't prevent him from wanting her more than ever.

Remembering what he'd said about the winner of the marble game getting to finish what they'd started in Gert's attic was no help at all. Swearing under his breath, he rose abruptly and stalked across the lot toward his apartment, very faintly hearing Amy asking Sarah if there was something wrong with him.

"I'll be back," he said over his shoulder.

Little did she know.

Chapter Thirteen

Three evenings later, Amy's doorbell rang. "Who is it?" she called.

"It's me. Sarah."

Sarah, alone? Surprised, Amy opened the door. "Come on in," she said.

Sarah slipped inside but wouldn't sit down. "I can't stay 'cause Daddy won't know where I am if he wakes up. He's taking a nap in front of the TV."

"Is something the matter?"

"It's about Betty. I keep telling Daddy, but he's sort of stopped listening. She can't come to violin lessons any more 'cause her mother had to have that operation and her father moved away, so they don't have any money."

"That's a shame," Amy said. "I'll call Mrs.

McBride right now and see if I can do something to help.''

"I miss Betty."

"Of course you do."

"I have to go in case Daddy wakes up." Sarah was out the door before Amy could say anything more.

When Cary answered the phone, her voice sounded so weak that Amy grew alarmed. "I heard you had an operation," she said. "Are you all right?"

"They had to take out my gallbladder. Everyone says recovery is so much easier with laser surgery, but I just can't seem to get back on my feet. And I have to, so I can go back to work."

There was no way Amy was going to pry into Cary's husband's absence. "What kind of work is it you do?"

"I'm a medical secretary for a Gardnerville group. I've already taken so much time off sick that I didn't have much left and it's up tomorrow." She began to cry.

That did it for Amy. Prying or not, she said bluntly, "Sarah says your husband moved out."

"Yes, he did." Cary spoke between sobs. "He hasn't sent us any money yet and I don't know when he will. There's the rent and food and Betty needs clothes for school." Her sobbing prevented her from going on.

"Hang in there while I see what I can do," Amy told her. Then she called Gert and explained the problem.

"A medical secretary? I just might have a solution for work. You know Eunice has been hinting she'd

like to retire so she and her husband can travel more
in their motor home. I wonder if Cary McBride would
be interested?''

Eunice was Gert's receptionist, and Amy knew she
was staying on only until Gert decided to find a re-
placement. "I can ask Cary," she said. "It'd be more
convenient for her to work right in town."

"Cary could come in part-time when she feels well
enough so that Eunice could orient her, and then go
full-time when she's recovered."

"Thanks, Gert. I'll let her know." Amy broke the
connection and stared down at the phone. Should she
risk calling David? She shrugged and punched in his
number. Since he was already angry with her, what
did it matter?

"Severin." He sounded a bit hoarse, as though the
call had roused him from his nap.

"This is Amy. I wondered if you knew what's happened to Betty's mother?" Without waiting for a response, she went on to tell him the problem, not saying Sarah had told her.

"So that's what Sarah was going on about," he
said. "I should have paid more attention."

"Gert's going to offer Cary a job," she said, hesitated, then plunged on—after all, he *was* a lawyer
even if he didn't intend to practice his profession. "Is
there any way you can think of to get her husband to
send her support money?"

"The feds have a dead-beat dad law on the books
to help the states find the guys and collect the money.
Nevada has its own law as well. I'll look into it."

She wanted to ask more questions to make him go

on talking, just to hear his voice, but forced herself
to end the call. "Thanks. I know Cary will appreciate
whatever you can do."

She sighed as she put the phone down, feeling more
bereft than she'd ever felt before—even after she'd
caught Vince with that graduate student. David's
businesslike tone of voice had convinced her it really
was over between them.

In the morning, David called Judge Maguire, found
he had some free time and dropped by to see him,
leaving Sarah in the waiting room with a book to
read.

"Nevada's got a damn good dead-beat dad law in
place," the judge told him. "With the Internet it's
easy enough to find the bastards these days. Collect-
ing is harder if there isn't a clear divorce settlement
where the child support amount is down in black and
white, but it's not impossible, even if he's still married but has taken off and isn't contributing to the
support of his children. The main problem is the
mothers don't know how to go about getting help to
force the men to pay up. No lawyer is going to make
a bundle pursuing dead-beat dads, so even if the
mothers can afford to hire one, few are interested."

At that moment David learned how it felt to have
an epiphany and the magnitude of it stunned him for
a moment. The judge was talking about dead-beat
dads who failed to supply their offspring with finan-
cial support. But what about David Severin? He'd
sent child support money without fail, but he'd never
so much as tried to support his daughter emotionally

until she was unexpectedly dumped in his lap. Wasn't he another kind of dead-beat dad?

Never mind that he'd made up for it as best he could once Sarah was with him, he'd been one in the past, and he was ashamed.

"You seem deep in thought," the judge said.

"I've decided to go after McBride," David said. "Once I locate him and force him to pay up, I'd appreciate it if you'd spread it around that there's now a local lawyer willing to take on all dead-beat dads in the area."

"You won't make a decent living," the judge warned.

David didn't feel it was necessary to tell him he didn't need the money, that he'd invested the inherited legacy from his grandfather and was living quite comfortably on the proceeds. "I'll get by," he said.

The judge shook his head. "Sooner you than me. If you're serious about this, contact the Child Support Enforcement Division, they field the complaints. I'll see that word gets around, too. God knows these poor women need help."

David collected Sarah from the waiting room and left, feeling as though he was walking on air. He'd found a goal, a lack that needed to be taken care of, one that he had the ability to help solve. In a way, it made him feel a bit less guilty for having neglected his own daughter for more than a year.

"I'm going to try to help Betty's mother collect money from Betty's father," he told Sarah.

"That's good. Then Betty'll come back to violin class. I miss her."

He explained that the money wouldn't arrive immediately—maybe not even soon, because they had to find Mr. McBride first. Sarah looked so disappointed that he added, "We'll find a way to get Betty back playing the violin."

As a start, when they returned home, he called Nell Archer and told her why Betty had dropped out. "Any suggestions?" he asked.

"What a shame," she said. "Maybe I can help by looking around for a scholarship or a grant. There are some for talented youngsters and Betty does have possibilities, just as your daughter does. What school does Betty go to?" When he told her, she added, "I'll begin there."

"Now," he said to Sarah, "here's what's happening. I'm working on getting money for Betty's mother to live on, Ms. Archer is going to try to find a way for Betty to go back to violin class and Gert is giving Betty's mother a job."

"Can I tell Amy when she gets home?" Sarah asked. "Or are you still mad at her?"

How in hell had she picked up on that? he wondered. "I'm not mad at Amy. We just aren't seeing as much of each other."

Sarah looked unconvinced. And sad.

"Okay, we'll both tell her tonight," he said.

She brightened. "Let's bring ice cream and chocolate syrup."

"What for?"

"'Cause then it'll sort of be like a party, and she'll know you're not mad at her anymore."

Deciding that, whatever Sarah thought about it, ice

cream and chocolate syrup wouldn't commit him to anything, David agreed.

Amy didn't arrive home at her usual time. Sarah, sitting outside with her father, said, "Maybe she's not coming."

"My guess is she stopped by to see Cary's mother." That'd be like Amy, whose sometimes tart tongue hid a soft heart.

"I forgot she stops to get stuff at that Chinese place. Maybe she did that, too."

When Amy finally drove up in her SUV and got out, David said to Sarah, "You're right. She's carrying a box from Wong's Palace."

Sarah jumped up and ran across the inner courtyard toward Amy, leaving David no choice but to trail after her. He reached the two of them as Sarah was asking, "Did you see Betty's mother?"

Amy nodded. "She's feeling better and hopes to come to work at Gert's office for a few hours on Monday. Betty said to say hello to you."

Turning to David, Sarah said, "So you were right, too, Daddy."

Nothing like a kid for putting you on the spot. "We've been waiting for you," he admitted.

"We put the ice cream in the fridge, but I'll go get it," Sarah volunteered, and was off across the courtyard before either of them could say anything.

"I was—that is, we were waiting to tell you more about Cary and Betty," David said.

"With ice cream?" The tartness was back in her voice.

"And chocolate syrup."

She nodded. "I see Sarah's hand in this." Glancing down at the box she carried, she added, "I over-bought, as usual, being a Chinese food junkie. There's plenty here for the three of us if you'd like to share."

Since he couldn't think of a reasonable excuse to refuse, he said yes. What had started out as a simple agreement with Sarah to tell Amy how he and Nell Archer were trying to help Cary and Betty, had some-how escalated into sharing dinner and dessert with her.

In Amy's apartment, Sarah finished eating first and asked if she could watch a Disney movie on the VCR.

"If it's okay with your dad," Amy said.

David nodded—what else could he do?

While they were eating, he'd told Amy about Nell Archer's plans to get Betty back in violin class, but not the dead-beat dad search, figuring Sarah was too young to hear about it in any detail.

Once Sarah was in the living room with the movie in progress, Amy said, "What about getting child support money from that rotten husband of Cary's?"

"Nevada's got a good dead-beat dad law on the books. I'll use it to go after McBride," he said.

Amy said nothing at all.

"You don't think that's a good idea?" he asked.

"Actually, I'm afraid to make a comment. You might misinterpret it."

He figured the tartness in her voice would curdle milk. Ignoring it, he said, "You know Cary better than I do. I plan to talk to her this weekend. Do you think she'll sign the necessary papers?"

"Would you like me to come with you?"

From past experience he knew getting wives to sign any kind of complaint against their husbands could be tricky. Having Amy, with her expertise, along with him might avoid that problem with Cary before it began. "Thanks. I'd appreciate it," he told her.

"If you're going to leave Sarah with Gert, maybe we should pick up Betty and bring her to Gert's, too. Whether he's a dead-beat or not, Betty loves her father and she shouldn't be around to maybe overhear the discussion."

"Betty loves a father who deserted her and her mother?" The minute the words were out, he shook his head. "Dumb question. If Sarah can love me despite what I did to her, then I can see that you're right about Betty. Gert won't mind an additional kid and Sarah will be happy to see Betty."

On Saturday, after Betty and Sarah were deposited at Gert's, David and Amy went back to Cary's house.

"I have to sign papers?" Cary asked after David had explained what he intended to do. "Gee, I don't know. Bill won't like that."

David glanced at Amy and she picked up the ball.

"Of course he won't," she said. "Your husband thinks he can get away with deserting his wife and child to spend his money elsewhere."

"Elsewhere?" Cary echoed. "You mean you think he's found another woman?"

Amy shrugged. "I have no idea. Many men do, though."

"I just thought he was tired of us and wanted to get away."

"Leaving you with no money but what you earn? Isn't that rather selfish when he knows it's not enough to cover all the expenses? Didn't he know you might need surgery?"

Cary bit her lip. "He sort of didn't want to know it."

Neither David nor Amy said anything for a time.

At last Cary sighed. "I have to think about Betty. It's not right for her to suffer, so I guess I will sign those papers."

"You're making the right choice," Amy assured her. "Betty is his daughter and he owes her as good a life as possible."

By the time they got ready to leave, Cary was looking less woebegone.

At the door, Amy said, "If it's all right with you, I'll pick up Betty tomorrow morning and take her with me to a barbecue at my brother's ranch in Carson Valley. Tell her to wear jeans, because she'll have the chance to ride a pony."

"That's kind of you. I know all this is upsetting her."

Though David made up his mind he wasn't going to comment, it troubled him that Sarah would be left out. By the time they reached his truck, he'd gone from troubled to annoyed.

"You didn't tell me about the barbecue," he muttered.

"Actually you and Sarah were invited," she said, "but I didn't think you'd care to go."

"And Sarah?"

She gave him a dark look. "I didn't think you'd

want her going anywhere with me," she said. "After all, I might try to psychoanalyze her."

A low shot, but he figured he'd earned it, so he merely said, "I don't feel that way. You've been good for Sarah." To his surprise, he found himself adding, "We'd both like to go to your brother's barbecue."

Only so Sarah can ride the pony, he tried to tell himself, but he knew he was lying. He'd badly missed Amy's company. And more.

Amy stared at him. "*You* want to go?"

"I don't see why we can't be friends." He knew it sounded lame, but there was nothing else he could think of. An apology was out of the question. He still felt betrayed.

"Well, of course you and Sarah can come," she said. "I'm not so sure about the rest of it."

Shut into the cab of the pickup with her, he could, ever so faintly, smell her floral scent, which made him remember other times with her. He closed his eyes for a moment, trying to banish the vision of her lying naked in his arms. Would he ever get over wanting her?

"Aren't you going to start the engine?" she asked.

More than anything, he needed to pull her into his arms and kiss her until the world went away.

"You're staring at me," she said, running a hand through her hair. "Have I got lipstick on my teeth or something awful like that?"

"I forgot your eyes were so green," he said inanely.

Amy shook her head. How was she supposed to

reply to something like that? Especially since the words sent a shiver of anticipation along her spine.

What's to anticipate? It's over and done with.

Yeah, and turtles can fly, shells and all. You still want the blasted man.

Since she couldn't seem to look away from him, she had to think of something to break the spell. "If you turn the key on," she said, "we could listen to music."

"What if that golden oldie Reno station is playing 'Dancing In The Dark'?"

He leaned closer as he spoke, having not yet fastened his seat belt. She had hers on so she couldn't scoot over closer to the door. Not that she could have moved, anyway. She could hardly even breathe. He was going to kiss her and she shouldn't let him, even though she thought she'd die if he didn't.

He eased over toward her. "Amy," he murmured, her name a caress. "Amy, I can't help it."

Neither could she. As much as the belt would let her, she leaned into his kiss and was lost. She wasn't even aware he'd unfastened her seat belt until he gathered her into his arms.

Never let me go. The thought pulsed through her, settling into her very bones.

She didn't know what might have happened if a convertible full of teenagers hadn't come by where they were parked along the curb, bass speakers throbbing, horn blaring. Catcalls from the teens brought them back to awareness. Amy pulled away, scooting over to her seat belt and fastening it again. David settled himself behind the wheel, put his on and turned the key in the ignition.

But he didn't drive toward Gert's or toward the apartment complex.

"Where are we going?" she asked finally.

"I can't take you home unless you want to face the consequences of us being there without the responsibility of Sarah. And I don't want to pick up the girls just yet. Not until we talk. The park by the river is fairly private, but not so much so I'll forget where we are again."

At the park, trails meandered along the river and to various picnic areas. They chose a river trail, but it soon became a single-file one, so when they came to a windfall with a substantial trunk alongside the trail, they sat on it, leaving a space between them. Though they'd seen others using the park, no one was in sight. The river gurgled past them—on its way to the Sink, Amy thought. To be swallowed up in the sand. The idea still disturbed her.

"No ducks here," she said.

"They know the picnic areas offer the best bet for handouts."

A magpie perched on a willow near them, flicking its tail while it eyed them.

"No food," Amy told the bird, holding out empty hands. As if understanding the words or the gesture, it flew away. She turned to David. "Well?"

"They run deep, I always heard."

She rolled her eyes at him. "Coming here was your idea."

"I'm having one hell of a time keeping my hands off you," he muttered.

Trying to ignore the thrill sending sparks through her at his admission, she said, "I noticed."

"You cooperated," he accused.

She could hardly deny it. "You're right, sorry to say."

"Do you know what I'm thinking right now?"

"That what's between us can lead nowhere?"

"Wrong. I'm trying to figure out if we'd be well enough hidden from the trail behind this windfall."

Dangerous though it might be, she couldn't resist teasing him. "Why would we want to hide?" she asked in her most innocent tone.

"Damn it, woman, be careful or I'll wind up showing you why."

Her breath came short as his gaze caught hers. What she saw in those blue eyes of his made her pulse pound. He was on a shorter leash than she'd thought.

"We can't." Even to herself she didn't sound convincing.

"We won't, maybe, but we sure as hell can. One touch and..."

He didn't need to finish. Every one of her nerve endings quivered with the need for him to touch her, kiss her, hold her. But she knew she was right about their relationship leading nowhere. She couldn't bear to think of making love with him knowing it might be for the last time.

Jumping to her feet, she cried, "We can't even discuss this rationally. It's time to go."

"Is it?" He rose slowly and took a step toward

her. She stood mesmerized. Another step. One more and she'd be in his arms. Lost.

"No!" she cried, whirling and fleeing down the trail toward the parking area.

Top: She held a crumpled veil, glancing alternately at it and the bit of heirloom tangled inside.

David—No, Dave, she had said. Not Mr. Coyote. Just call me Dave, and call me—

Chapter Fourteen

David and Amy rode in silence most of the way to the apartment complex, their only conversation about the barbecue on Sunday. She wanted to drive alone, but he convinced her Sarah and Betty would make more than adequate chaperones. He dropped her off and, his mind in turmoil, drove to Gert's to pick up the girls.

Both Sarah and Betty were thrilled to discover they'd be going to a barbecue together the next day and jabbered to each other all the way to Betty's. On the way home, though, Sarah lapsed into silence, which was unlike her.

"Tired, punkin?" he asked.

"No, I'm thinking."

He smiled. That was a new one. "About what?"

"About what Great-aunt Gert said."

He waited, but she didn't divulge any more. "What was that?" he asked finally.

She turned solemn eyes on him. "I'm not finished thinking yet."

"So you're not going to tell me until you are?"

She nodded.

What a joy his daughter was. Always something different going on in her head. He couldn't for the life of him understand why he'd more or less deserted her for so long. It'd never happen again.

"You took Amy home first," she said.

"She had things to do."

Again she examined him, this time with what he'd come to recognize as her "are you sure?" look.

"She's coming with us tomorrow?"

He nodded.

That evening all three of the new owners came to pick up their kittens, leaving only Sheba, who cuddled up to her mother as though afraid she'd be next.

"Is Hobo going to have more kittens?" Amy asked.

"Don't you remember I told you Hobo has to go to the vet so he can fix it so she won't have kittens? When Sheba gets a little older, we'll take her, too."

"Will Hobo care?"

"No. She won't even realize anything is different. Cats are smart, but their brains work differently from ours. She'll be healthier afterward and live longer, too."

"Oh. I guess I won't feel sorry for her, then."

"No need to. And Sheba is so small it's better for her if she never has kittens."

"She's got me to love," Sarah said, picking up the kitten, who immediately started purring. "Love is important, Great-aunt Gert told me."

"Is that what you've been thinking about?"

Sarah took a while to answer. "Sort of."

On Sunday, the four of them left in midmorning, driving in David's pickup.

"There'll be other kids at the barbecue," Amy told Sarah and Betty.

"Boys or girls?" Sarah asked.

"Both."

Viewing his daughter in the rearview mirror, David could see the news disturbed her. "You like Elias, don't you?" he said.

"He's younger than me, so he's okay."

Thinking back, he remembered her talking about a boy back in New Mexico who'd made fun of her. Evidently Amy recalled it, too, because she spoke before he'd figured out what to say.

"All boys aren't bullies like Kenny," Amy said.

She even knew the kid's name, which was more than he did.

"Kenny needs help to understand why he picks on others," she continued, "but the boys coming to my brother's aren't like that. Some are about your age, some younger. You have to be careful not to judge all boys by one bad one. Think about it, your dad was once a boy and I'm sure he never bullied anyone."

He could see Sarah struggling to assimilate this and wondered if her thoughts ran like this: *Daddy a boy?*

Never! He hadn't been able to imagine his lawyer father as a boy. Grandpa, yes, his dad, no.

"*He* might have been a bully," Sarah said.

For a moment David thought she meant him, but then he realized the emphasis on "he" meant Murdock. He didn't intend to defend the bastard.

"I know you don't like your stepfather," Amy said. "Now that you're living with your father, though, you don't have to hate Mr. Murdock anymore."

"I don't?"

"Certainly not. Why should you? You're happy here, you don't have to live with him anymore, so you can give up hating him."

"Okay, I'll try." Sarah sounded dubious.

"I like some boys at school," Betty said.

This seemed to reassure Sarah a little, but by now David was trying to remember if he'd ever bullied anyone. He may have tried with his sister, but she was a fighter from the beginning. How could Amy be so sure he hadn't been a bully?

They arrived early at Russ and Mari's ranch, but a few others were already there. David immediately recognized Zed Adams, his wife, Karen, son, Danny, and daughter, Erin. As it turned out Amy had met the Adamses, too, so only Sarah and Betty needed to be introduced.

"We've been waiting for you to come," Danny said, "so we could go ride the ponies. Elias is already down there. Come on."

Erin and Betty started right off with him, but Sarah

hung back until Amy whispered something in her ear, then away she went.

"What did you tell her?" David asked.

"That Danny might be as tall as she was, but he was younger."

Smiling at each other, they shared the moment, making David realize how much it meant to him that Amy cared about Sarah, too.

Russ said, "David, barbecue rules in the Valley are the men do the outside cooking, the women the inside. Right now, what say we go down and help Hank with the pony rides."

David nodded and the three men followed the children, leaving the women behind.

"I cheated," Mari confessed. "My housekeeper and Willa—you both remember her—did most of the 'inside' work already. Let's go up to the house and relax while we can. It gets hectic later on with everyone here and kids all over the place."

"Is Willa still raising rattlesnakes and milking their venom?" Karen asked.

Rattlesnakes? Amy only vaguely recalled Willa—an older woman—since they'd met just once, at Russ and Mari's wedding.

"No, Grandpa Joe really took to Willa, you know. He claims she's the only person he's ever met who tells the truth, bad or good, one hundred percent of the time and can still make him smile when it's bad. He finally persuaded her to let the snakes go. After he took over her investments, she did so well, she really didn't need the money she got for the venom."

They passed the gazebo on the way to the house

and Amy paused to look at it. "David's aunt is having him build her a gazebo in her backyard," she said. "They're so romantic. I'm looking forward to eating lunch inside it when he's finished."

Karen and Mari both laughed.

"Sorry," Mari said, "but *romantic* and *lunch* don't exactly go together. Unless you mean you and David having a midnight snack in the gazebo."

Amy forced a smile.

In the house, Willa, who was holding baby Isabel, greeted Karen, then surveyed Amy. "Met you at the wedding. Still steering clear of men?"

Taken aback, Amy took a moment to recover. How on earth had Willa figured that out?

"Actually, she and David Severin are friends," Mari said.

Willa nodded. "Glad to hear it. At my age you can take men or leave 'em alone, but a young gal like you, it's different, worth the hurt that goes along with the joy."

Joe was right, Willa didn't mince words. But worth the hurt? No way. To take the focus off her, Amy said, "Do you mind if I hold my niece?"

"Best she gets to know her aunt early," Willa said, depositing Isabel in Amy's arms.

"Isn't she darling?" Karen said after they'd all sat down. "You Simons have the most beautiful green eyes."

Amy remembered how David had compared the color of her eyes to the green of Emerald Bay and had to hold back a sigh. Why must everything remind her of that night with David?

"I've met Gert Severin," Karen said. "She's a remarkable woman and I'm sure you enjoy being her associate."

"She's great to work with."

"You mentioned David building a gazebo for her. Has he decided to resume his law practice?"

Amy chose her words carefully. "I don't think so."

Karen looked from Amy to Mari. "I guess neither of you knew him then, but a year or so ago, *morose* was the word best fitting David. How he's changed for the better!" She smiled at Amy.

Amy couldn't believe her ears. Karen thought *she* was responsible for his change?

Isabel cooed, attracting Amy's attention. Looking down at the baby, she wondered if a child of hers would have green eyes, too. If she ever had one. How good it felt to cuddle her niece next to her. It might be only an instinctive reaction, but feeling it made her better understand why women yearned to have babies.

"When is Talal due back from Kholi?" Mari asked Karen.

"Not till next month." Evidently realizing Amy didn't know who Talal was, she added, "Talal is Zed's twin brother and Danny's birth father." She laughed. "Danny always brags he's got two fathers, because Zed and I are raising him. Now that she's old enough to understand, it annoys Erin no end when he teases her about only having one."

More guests arrived, including Zed's sister Jade and her family. The men and older children all went outside, while the women gathered in the huge living room with the toddlers and babies.

"Is everyone here related to everyone else?" Amy asked Mari.

"Not exactly, though a lot of them have ties to Zed and Karen in one way or another."

By the time the men finished the barbecuing outside, the women had set the rest of the food out on tables in the vast screened porch to the side of the house. Despite children underfoot and running in and out, everyone managed to eat. After the cleanup, Jade brought out her guitar and they sat around singing folk songs.

The camaraderie made Amy nostalgic for summers on Mackinac Island when she was small. She'd loved her father then. He had, she remembered, called her Kitten. She hadn't thought about that in years.

Russ was sitting close to her so she leaned over and said, "Do you remember when Mother used to play the piano and we'd all sing?"

He nodded. "On the island. Seems ages ago. Dad always said you were the only one who could carry a tune."

"He did?" She had no memory of that.

"You could never do wrong in Dad's eyes. Made it hard on me. If you teased me I didn't dare clobber you like you deserved or Dad got after me."

"He changed his mind about me later on, when I wouldn't do what he wanted. Dad's always been into control. You know that."

"He's mellowed."

She shot him a disbelieving glance.

Ignoring that, he said, "I doubt you need my approval, but here it is, anyway—David's okay."

"I knew you ex-lawyers would stick together."

"He's not ex, he passed the Nevada bar exams."

"His aunt Gert nagged him into it."

"From what I've seen of him I doubt David is easily nagged into anything." He gave her an assessing look. "You haven't been trying any of your covert maneuvering with him, have you?"

"Of course not."

"Why don't I believe that? Cease and desist, sister of mine. He's not the type to stand for anyone trying to control him by whatever means."

Control David? Before she could tell Russ he was out of his mind, Mari claimed his attention and the chance was gone. Control? Why, she'd never tried to control anyone in her life. "Never," she repeated aloud.

"Never what?" David asked from behind her.

He hadn't been there before, so he must have just come up to her. Thank heaven he hadn't overheard her exchange with her brother. "Never mind," she said.

"Ready to leave?" he asked.

"We'll have to collect Betty and Sarah."

"They're in the games room trying to learn Ping-Pong from one of the teenagers Russ and Mari hired to keep track of the kids. They're having fun, so we can give them a few more minutes while we take a walk."

"A walk where?"

"Outside, like a lot of others are doing."

In other words, they wouldn't be alone. "All right."

With the waning moon hovering between half and quarter full, the night was quite dark once they moved away from the lighted areas. Other couples strolled along meandering paths where the night breeze, laden with a heavy, sweet scent, dissipated the day's heat.

"I think I smell night-blooming jasmine," she said.

"Gert wanted me to plant some against her back fence, but after Cal told me it usually doesn't survive northern Nevada winters, she decided against it. The odor's a tad strong for me. I prefer something lighter, like—" He broke off.

"Like what?"

"It doesn't matter."

"Then why not tell me?"

He stopped, took hold of her shoulders and turned her toward him. "Damn it, the floral scent I prefer is the one you wear." Without giving her a chance to free herself, he brought his mouth down on hers, hard and demanding. Hungry.

A part of her had known all along if she agreed to walk with him she'd wind up in his arms. The same part of her that longed to be there. The irresponsible, "take joy where you find it and never mind tomorrow" part. That part of herself she'd kept on a tight leash ever since her experience with Vince. Somehow David had not only untied the leash, but thrown it away.

Unable to control herself, she fed his hunger with her own. To the devil with moon love. Her love for David was no moonlight illusion, but deep and real. They might have no future, but he was kissing her in the here and now and so she'd answer his passion with hers.

Finally, without letting her go, he lifted his head slightly and said against her lips, "The more I kiss you, the more I want. But..." Leaving it unfinished, he set her free from his embrace.

Going home in the truck, they had little to say to each other. She listened to the two girls in back rehashing the evening.

"Who did you like the best?" Betty said. "Of the boys, I mean."

"I guess Danny. He's fun."

"I liked Tim better. Danny's bossy."

"Yeah, but if you don't do what he says he doesn't get mad. He's not mean."

Amy shook her head. Seven years old and already discussing boys. Oh well, at least Sarah had come to realize not every boy is a bully.

As they chattered on, Amy's eyes closed and she drifted off to sleep.

When David stopped the pickup to see Betty to the door of her place, he tried to be quiet so he wouldn't wake Amy. Back in the truck, he saw she still slept. She didn't rouse when he reached the apartment complex, either.

Sarah peered over into the front seat and said, "Are you going to carry her in like you did me the other night?"

"She might not appreciate that."

"I liked it."

"I didn't know you were awake enough to tell what was going on."

"I was only sort of awake, but I knew. I bet she'd like being carried. It makes you feel real safe."

He smiled at her. So many times his daughter's words touched his heart. "Amy isn't you, punkin."

"No, but she's a girl."

He was saved further protests when Amy stirred, opened her eyes and said, "I must have fallen asleep. Are we home?"

"I told Daddy he should carry you upstairs," Sarah said, "but he didn't think you'd like it. I told him you would."

"I'll have to think about that," Amy told her after a short pause. "I'm awake now, so I can make it on my own." She unbuckled her seat belt. "Good night all."

As Sarah and David headed for their apartment, she said, "It still isn't fixed."

"What isn't?"

"You know." And she wouldn't say any more.

Sarah started school on Monday, and, without her "helping" him build Aunt Gert's gazebo, the work went faster. Tuesday he took Hobo to the vet's to be spayed and brought her home the same day. By Friday he had the floor of the gazebo in and had finished the steps. But he hadn't even caught a glimpse of Amy all week.

He had nothing planned except hanging out with Sarah for the weekend, which was just as well, because it rained. After her violin class on Saturday, he got out some of the games they'd bought during the summer.

"It'd be more fun if there were four of us," Sarah said. "I could ask Amy and then we could all go over to Great-aunt Gert's. I bet she'd like to play."

"How about Betty?"

She frowned. "Daddy, you should listen better. I told you Betty had to go somewhere with her mother."

"Sorry." And he was. He'd been absentminded lately.

"So can I ask Amy?"

He gave in. "Okay, you ask Amy, but first let me tell Gert we're coming over."

"Sounds good to me," Gert told him. "You can have supper here."

He told Sarah. She punched in Amy's number and, despite himself, he tensed. She might be out. Or refuse.

"Hi, this is Sarah."

So she was home.

"Daddy and I need you to play some games with us over at Great-aunt Gert's. She invited us to eat supper, too. You can ride with us if you want."

He figured she wouldn't go that far. But would she come at all?

"Oh. Okay, then we'll go by ourselves, too."

Bingo.

When they got to Gert's she already had a round card table set up in the living room. "I haven't played Monopoly in more years than I care to remember," she said.

"I just started playing it," Sarah said. "There's lots to remember, but it's not very hard."

"Is Amy coming?" Gert asked.

"By herself," Sarah said.

Gert raised her eyebrows but didn't comment.

They began the game after Amy arrived. Gert so consistently lost that David suspected she was deliberately giving Sarah chances to win. After two games Gert insisted she couldn't go on without popcorn.

"No help needed," she said. "It's microwave."

When she left the room a silence fell, broken by Sarah's plaintive voice. "I wish you two were friends."

"We are," Amy said.

"Not like before. I thought maybe it's on account of me, but Great-aunt Gert says no. In case it is, though, it's okay with me if you want to get married."

The two of them stared at her, stunned.

"Danny told me about having two fathers. I asked him if he loved them both and he said sure. I only want one father, but it'd be awesome to have two mothers, 'cause I love Amy just like I do Mommy. It'd be fun to have Amy living with us, don't you think so, Daddy?"

Gert, who'd come back into the room, said, "Out of the mouth of babes. I told Sarah she's got the makings of a great shrink." She motioned to Sarah. "But right now I need your help in the kitchen."

Left alone with Amy, David had his second epiphany of the year. His daughter was right. He needed Amy in every way possible. Needed her as his wife.

He grinned at her. "Kind of a shock, but she has something there. What are the odds I'll make a better husband than a patient?"

As she tried to comprehend his words, what her brother had said to her at the barbecue flashed through her mind. *Covert maneuvering. Trying to control David.* Her eyes widened as she realized the truth. She *had* tried to do that, tried to control David, to make him do what she thought he should. Why, she was as bad as her father! Shocked at the revelation, she bolted from the room, out of the house and into her SUV.

Unable to bring herself to go home, she drove aimlessly around for what seemed to be hours, too upset for tears.

Chapter Fifteen

Gert reassured Sarah that Amy was all right, then settled her in the TV room with popcorn and limeade before she'd allow David to say a word. Gert had also ordered him not to go after Amy until they talked things over. He paced impatiently, knowing Gert was right but increasingly worried about Amy.

As soon as Gert came back into the room, he began, "All I said to her was did she think I'd make a better husband than a patient. Why would that upset her?"

"I'm not sure. What would those words mean to Amy?"

He explained how he'd accused her more than once of trying to psychoanalyze him. "She told me I wasn't facing that I was in denial. Shrink lingo. I told her to cut it out. She agreed, but she broke her word. I got ticked off.''

"Do you think you were in denial?"

He shook his head. "Amy kept interpreting every legal matter I took on as facing down my denial. She was wrong. I had no incentive to return to practice until I found out from Judge Maguire the tremendous problem dead-beat dads are in this state. What I needed all along was a cause—and I found one.''

"Did you tell her this?"

"Not yet. We haven't been on good terms.''

"So Sarah told me when she asked my advice last week. I told her the two of you needed confronting, explaining to her what that was.''

"No wonder she wouldn't tell me what she was thinking about.''

"You can't blame her. It took a lot of courage for Sarah to speak out.''

"I know." He sighed. "I thought I was in love with Iris but realized too late that wasn't what it was.''

"I'm afraid poor Iris hasn't learned how to love.''

"So how was I supposed to understand what it was I felt for Amy?"

"As Grandfather would say, 'Trust your heart.'"

"That's not much help now. Do you have any idea what upset Amy?"

"I believe what you said to her about being a better husband than a patient triggered something hidden within her—shooting it out to confront her. She fled because she needed to be alone to come to terms with it. That's why I told you not to rush after her. She needs time and so do you. I want you to sit down and go over everything that's happened between you and Amy since you met. The bad and the good. Somewhere in there you'll find a clue to how you need to behave when you meet again."

With reluctance he dropped onto a loveseat.

"I'll bring you some popcorn and limeade, then I'm going in to watch TV with Amy. When you come up with the right answer, let me know."

He didn't want to sit and think, nor eat popcorn, he wanted to find Amy. Gert, though, was no fool. And it was true he didn't have a plan.

Gert returned, set the popcorn and limeade on the end table beside him, hesitated, then crossed to the small purple CD player she'd bought for Sarah. "Music sometimes helps," she said. She shuffled through a few CDs, shook her head, opened a cabinet, brought out a multi-CD holder and chose one of the CDs. "I have a feeling sentimental songs from my era will work better than Sarah's wailing rock stars," she said as she inserted the disk into the player.

"You're too tense. Lean back and close your eyes," she ordered before leaving.

He tried his best to relax, not paying much attention to the background music as he struggled to go back to the beginning.

He'd wanted Amy even before he'd known who she was, and, from her reaction to him then, he suspected she'd felt the zing between them, too. The zing had intensified as they got better acquainted, becoming impossible to ignore. But at the same time he'd begun to *like* Amy. By the time Sarah arrived he'd been captivated, at least sexually.

Her warm acceptance of his daughter and her unobtrusive way of boosting Sarah's self-image had warmed his heart. He understood now he'd been a damn fool not to understand what was happening to him.

There'd been the camel ride and all the other excursions the three of them had taken. *As a family, you idiot.* How could he have been so blind?

"Come dance with me," a tenor sang, and the words catapulted him back to the deck of the *Frivolous*, dancing with Frivolous Amy in his arms. A night he'd never forget as long as he lived. Thanks to old Joe Haskell.

Haskell must be almost a contemporary of Gert's. No wonder the music sounded familiar. As Gert had said, the songs were sentimental. Romantic.

Romantic. Amy had arranged a romantic night for them to discover the depth of what was between them. What had he ever done for her that was romantic?

"Moonlight becomes you," another man sang, a baritone this time. Which reminded David of Amy's definition of moon love as not the real thing. He knew what the real thing was now, all right, and it damn well better not be too late.

That's when he had a third epiphany. Leaping to his feet, he rushed to the CD holder, pulling out each CD and reading the label on both sides. He found what he wanted on the last one. He shut off Sarah's purple CD player, removed the CD, inserted the new one, turned it back on and, jiggling with impatience, let it play until the song he wanted came on. Shutting it off again, he disconnected the cord from the player—luckily it was a battery player—picked up the purple case and called to Gert.

"Do me a favor."

She came into the room. "Of course."

"I figured out what to do. After you put Sarah to bed upstairs, would you call Amy and ask her to come back over here? I don't care how you do it, but get her to go out to the gazebo."

"It's unfinished."

"No problem, the floor's in."

Gert raised her eyebrows.

"Romance," he said. "Trust me."

She nodded. "And where will you be?"

"First I have to move the truck so Amy won't see it here. Then I'll just be waiting."

"You realize it'll be a while."

He sighed. "You might say I deserve a long wait."

"Yes, in the truck, wherever you park it," Gert told him. "That way I won't have to tell too many lies to Amy."

Amy finally stopped her aimless wandering and drove home. As she parked, she noticed David's truck wasn't in its place. Good. The last thing she wanted was for him to come knocking on her door.

She hadn't had anything to eat since lunch, but food had no appeal to her. Aware she'd have a problem sleeping, though, she warmed milk and made a piece of toast to go with it.

After considering whether or not to turn on the TV,

she decided against it, ate the toast, drank the milk and sat brooding. The way might have been roundabout, but David had asked her to marry him and she'd run out of Gert's house like some brain-fried nutcase. What must he think? That he'd insulted her? She sighed. The truth was much worse. She'd fled because she'd uncovered an unacceptable truth about herself. How could she ever face him again?

When the phone rang she checked the caller ID and saw the number was Gert's. She hesitated—it might be David—but finally picked up the phone on the chance it could be Gert.

"Amy, I need you to come over here," Gert said.

"Is David there?"

"Sarah's upstairs sleeping, but David's gone."

Alarm struck Amy. Where had he gone? Not home. She'd been compulsively checking his slot, the last time only a few minutes ago, and his truck hadn't been in it. Surely David was too levelheaded to do anything foolish. Wasn't he?

"I'll be right over," she said.

On the way, she decided Gert must want to talk to her about what happened. She really didn't want to, but she owed Gert some kind of explanation.

David's truck wasn't in the driveway. Not that she'd thought Gert wasn't telling the truth, but after all, he was her nephew. When Gert let her in, Amy noticed she was hobbling.

"Are you all right? What happened to you?" she asked.

"I tripped and twisted my ankle after I put Sarah to bed. I really hated to bother you, but, before I injured my ankle, I promised her I'd bring her that purple CD player that she left out on the floor of the gazebo. I simply can't make it out there to get it and I hate to disappoint her. I'm sorry to disturb you after whatever happened earlier, but I decided after you bring in the CD player we can talk.''

Amy had known the talk would be somewhere on Gert's agenda. "You should be sitting with your foot elevated and ice on that ankle," she scolded.

"That's where I'll be when you come back in."

As she headed for the dark backyard, Amy thought of returning to her SUV for a flashlight but shook her head. The moon's light, though dim, would be enough to locate the player, and Tourmaline was practically crime-free compared to any community in California.

Did she hear music? It was so faint the sound must be coming from the house up the block, coming through open windows. It wasn't until she was almost to the unfinished gazebo that she recognized the tune. Just as the singer began his solo, David's voice froze her in her tracks.

"Ms. Frivolous," he said, "may I have this dance?"

The next she knew, he'd grasped her hand, led her up the steps onto the gazebo floor, and then she was in his arms, dancing in the dark. He didn't say a word as he swung her around and around. With the memory of the first time they'd danced like this overwhelming her, all she could do was follow where he led. Gert had lied to her, but she didn't care, nothing mattered except David.

When the song ended, another she recognized began. "This isn't moon love," he whispered in her ear. "This is true love. I do love you, Amy." He danced her over to the steps, then pulled her down to sit beside him.

"I've found my place as a lawyer," he told her. "I'll be helping women find dead-beat dads, like Betty's."

Amy promptly burst into tears. He put his arm around her, letting her weep onto this chest. When at last she'd cried herself out, he offered her a bandanna to mop her face, telling her, "Lucky us yardmen always carry bandannas."

"Do you know what I tried to do to you?" she asked, pulling away from him to sit up straight.

"Tell me."

"I've been trying all along to control you. I'm just like my f-father." Her voice broke, but she fought back more tears. "My only excuse is that I didn't realize what I was doing until today."

"Until I asked you to marry me. Is that what was wrong? Hey, no problem. You didn't succeed—I made my own decision. Actually I'm as uncontrollable as you are. I'll take my chances with you if you're willing to take your chances with me."

"You taught me to take chances again," she told him. "And I've loved you for what seems like forever. Why wouldn't I want to marry you?"

Pulling her to her feet, he stepped back onto the floor and, holding her in his arms, danced with her as a tenor sang about racing with the moon. "This gingerbread man is through running," he murmured, stopping. She raised her face, eager for his kiss. Just before his lips met hers, he whispered, "I remembered to bring a quilt, so don't worry about splinters."

And then they were lost in each other.

Chapter Sixteen

Two months later, they were married in the completed gazebo with Sarah as the proud flower girl, Gert as the matron of honor and Russ as best man. At the last minute, David's sister Diane flew in from Hawaii, barely in time for the ceremony, but a wonderful surprise. The only disappointment was Amy's father, who, because of an emergency appendectomy, couldn't get there.

Because he knew Amy needed to connect with her father, David made up his mind to remedy the situation.

His chance didn't come for more than six months, when Nell Archer scheduled a violin recital for her pupils.

The recital was held in an old theater building that no longer showed movies. The building had escaped destruction, because in Gold Rush years it had been an opera house, which gave it a place on the historic registry. The children had been rehearsing on the stage for several weeks, so no longer were in awe of their surroundings.

Sarah's group of attendees included David, Amy, Gert and Grandfather, as well as Mari and Russ. Brent and Iris Murdock had been invited as well, but had sent regrets from Bermuda. As the group was about to get settled in their seats, an older man strode down the aisle toward them.

Amy couldn't believe her eyes. "Dad?"

Lou Simon wrapped her in a bear hug. "David called to invite me," he said after he let her go. "That damn appendix made me miss your wedding, but I wasn't going to miss this. It's not every day a man gets a bonus granddaughter who's a violin virtuoso."

When the curtains parted, he sat down next to Amy. David was on the other side of her and she leaned over to whisper "Thank you" in his ear.

Sarah not only had a duet with Betty, but a violin solo as well. Through her own tears, Amy noticed David's misty eyes as he watched his daughter perform. *Their* daughter. Sarah was as much her child as the one growing inside her.

After the performance, punch and cookies were served in the theater anteroom for the audience and violinists. As they stood in a group, Sarah joined them, Betty and her mother tagging behind. Cary singled out David.

"I can't thank you enough for what you've done," she said. "So far the money comes in from him every month and it's such a relief. Why, Betty wouldn't even have been in this recital if it hadn't been for you.''

Invited to join them, Cary shook her head. "Thanks, but we're with friends.''

As Cary and Betty moved away, Amy saw her father crouch down and hold out his hand to Sarah. "I'm your Grandpa Lou,'' he said. "I'll give you a hug if that's okay with you.''

Instead of replying, Sarah reached out and hugged him. "Daddy said you were coming, but we kept it a secret from Mom so she'd be surprised.''

Lou straightened. "That was a fine performance,'' he said. "You're a talented girl.''

Amy hugged Sarah, saying, "I think so, too. I'm so proud of you, honey.''

Lou put an arm around Amy. "I'm proud of you, too, kitten,'' he told her. "Both you and Russ proved me wrong about what I thought was best for you. Taught me a lesson. I promise I'll try not to enforce my will on this one here—'' he touched Sarah's head "—or any of my other grandchildren.''

Someday I'll tell him that I have the same failing, Amy thought. Thank heaven we both realized the problem before it was too late.

"What's 'enforce your will'?'' Sarah asked.

"It means someone trying to make you do things you may not want to do,'' Amy said. "Not necessary things for your health or safety, those are for your own good, but if I tried to make you play the piano instead of the violin, I'd be enforcing my will on you because I didn't take into consideration what you wanted to play.''

"Oh. Like boarding school.''

Oops. Smart kid. In a way, Sarah was right, but someday she'd have to come to terms with the fact her birth mother was married to a man whose own convenience came first. It would take time.

"Your stepfather likes to travel," Amy said. "That's why boarding school came up. In his own way, he was trying to find a safe place for you while he and your mother were gone." Lame, but it was all she could think of offhand.

"I made a tape of your solo and the duet with Betty," David told Sarah. "I'll send a copy to them when they get back from Bermuda so they'll be able to play it and be proud of you, too.''

Sarah, leaning against Amy, nodded. She gently patted Amy's enlarging abdomen and said, "We can play the tape for the baby, too, so he can listen to me playing. Ms. Archer says you're never too young to enjoy music.''

"So you know the one coming is a boy?" Lou asked.

"That's what the docs tell us," David said.

As her father and David continued to talk, it suddenly struck Amy what she wanted to name the baby. She bent over and whispered in Sarah's ear.

"Awesome," Sarah said. She tugged at Lou's hand. "Know what, Grandpa? Mom's going to name the baby Louis, after you. But I think maybe I'll call him Louie.''

Lou chuckled, tears in his eyes.

Amy looked at David and he took her hand, running his thumb caressingly over hers, his touch telling her without words how much he loved her.

What a fool she'd been to think that love could ever be controlled!

*   *   *   *   *

Coming in May 2002

**Three Bravo men marry for convenience—
but will they love in leisure? Find out in
Christine Rimmer's *Bravo Family Ties!***

Cash—for stealing a young woman's innocence, and to
give their baby a name, in *The Nine-Month Marriage*

Nate—for the sake of a codicil in his beloved
grandfather's will, in *Marriage by Necessity*

Zach—for the unlucky-in-love rancher's chance to
have a marriage—even of convenience—
with the woman he *really* loves!

BRAVO
FAMILY TIES

Where love comes alive™

These New York Times *bestselling authors
have created stories to capture the hearts and minds
of women everywhere.
Here are three classic tales about the power of love—
and the wonder of discovering the place
where you belong....*

FINDING HOME

DUNCAN'S BRIDE
by
LINDA HOWARD

CHAIN LIGHTNING
by
ELIZABETH LOWELL

POPCORN AND KISSES
by
KASEY MICHAELS

*Available only from Silhouette
at your favorite retail outlet.*

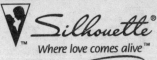

Silhouette®
Where love comes alive™

Visit Silhouette at www.eHarlequin.com   PSFH